Life, According to Whom

Freshman Year

Ashley M. King

Get It Done Publishing

Contents

Chapter One

They voted me out and gave us sixty days."

"Sixty days?"

"—and that was kind of them," he stated. "They only gave us more time due to Sara being in school and it being this close to the end of the school year."

"I just can't, can't believe this."

"We tried, Elaine. I tried, and now this is all in God's hands. I fought my good fight and stood on the side of truth, but—Lord willing."

John was at a loss for words. He had been preaching for 34 years without a spot or blemish to his name, 11 of those at his current church. If anyone knew John, they would say he was a righteous, honest, family man. So, it shook the community and the board members when rumors flew that Pastor John was having an affair with a church member—a married one at that.

The sad part about it is that John was the last to find out about this supposed affair. A few weeks ago, Elaine, John's wife of thirty-one years, was at the grocery store when one of the members of the church came up to her and said, "I'm sorry to hear what you're going through, but know that we are praying for you. I just can't believe it, Elaine, and with all people, the mayor's wife."

Clueless about what the lady was talking about, Elaine apologized for not knowing what she meant. The lady gasped and walked off, realizing she had spilled the beans. Elaine stood there for a few seconds, gathering her thoughts, dismissed the encounter, and finished her shopping.

It wasn't until Sara got home that things began to unfold.

"Dad!" Sara yelled, slamming the door. "Daaaaaaaaad!"

"Everything alright?" Her dad managed to ask as he sprinted across the house.

"You didn't? Did you?"

"Didn't do what?"

"Sara, what's going on?" her mom asked, sitting at the table, noticing the flush in her face and the water gathering in her eyes.

"Dad, I don't believe it—" sniffling and doing a poor job of holding back her tears.

"Believe what?" he asked.

"That you had an affair with Mrs. Talsburt?"

"A what? An affair?"

"An affair?" echoed Elaine.

"Everyone at school is talking about it. I wasn't sure what everyone was snickering about and pointing at until my friends came up to me and told me that they were 'sorry' to hear what my father had done! And asked me if I was okay."

Realizing what had transpired at the grocery store, Elaine held onto a chair to regain her balance. She was suddenly overtaken by nausea. She inhaled and exhaled deep breaths. John, not believing what he had heard, reassured his wife and daughter that he didn't have an affair, and clearly, there must be a grave misunderstanding.

Pastor John and Elaine had counseled Mr. and Mrs. Talsburt months ago, regarding their marriage and trust in one another. Mr. Talsburt, so happened to be the town's mayor and a very busy one at that. Mrs. Talsburt felt left out of his life and was only asked to be in the picture when it was time for photo-ops. Mrs. Talsburt stated that it wasn't like that at first. Mr. Talsburt was charming, debonair, and would woo her off her feet when they were courting. She enjoyed the chase, and that slowly faded over time. Instead of being his trophy on his arm, she became the trophy on the wall, forgotten about, collecting dust.

Pastor John and Elaine listened to both sides and gave feedback. Pastor John informed Mr. Talsburt that work had become his wife and suggested that he and Mrs. Talsburt start dating again. Dating just like they did when they first met. Mr. Talsburt would need to schedule these dates, just as he did everything else on his calendar, to show how serious he was about keeping his marriage. Mr. Talsburt felt they were taking Mrs. Talsburt's side, but he agreed. Elaine suggested once a week, but Mr. Talsburt rebutted that his schedule was too demanding and that he would commit to every other week. Mrs. Talsburt smiled and was happy with the outcome.

Pastor assumed everything was going well since it had been two months since he'd heard from either one of them, until Mrs. Talsburt dropped by the church unannounced. Pastor heard a knock at his door and assumed it was his admin, so he said, "Come in" without looking up. It was Mrs. Talsburt. The admin had stepped away, given that there were no appointments on the Pastor's schedule for the time being.

Mrs. Talsburt looked distraught, crying so hard that her nose was red. Seeing that she wasn't entirely herself, "Sit down, Mrs. Talsburt," Pastor encouraged. "What's wrong? What has you all in tears?"

Mrs. Talsburt began to pour out her heart. Caught off guard by Mrs. Talsburt's emotional appearance, Pastor did not close his door. Generally, when Pastor is counseling, particularly the opposite sex, he has someone in the room with him, but not this day. When the admin, Tessa, came back to her desk, her ears got a mouthful, or at least what she could make out with the background noise.

It's apparent to Tessa that whoever is in the Pastor's office is an emotional wreck. She overheard the lady tell her husband she was out to lunch with some friends, even though she knew she was coming to see him. And that she was tired of all the secrets and holding onto the guilt of this affair. She wanted to be honest with her husband, but she knew what it would do to him and their family. Having heard enough to come to her own conclusion, Tessa figured she would leave her desk as quietly and slowly as she could, to give the two privacy while staying close enough to see who this mystery woman was.

After about twenty minutes of lurking behind the scenes, the mystery lady had come forth out of the office to reveal unto her that it was Mrs. Talsburt. Tessa waited about three minutes after Mrs. Talsburt left to return to her desk. Not sure what to do with this information, she sat on it.

It was days later when the Pastor delivered a sermon on fidelity. Tessa observed Mrs. Talsburt excuse herself in the middle of the sermon and took that as an admission of guilt, interpreting the Pastor's sermon as a veiled confession. She felt obligated to report this information to the board members.

Clearly, the information somehow leaked out before a meeting with the Pastor. A few weeks ago, the Pastor was summoned to a board meeting when these allegations were brought to him. Given who Mrs. Talsburt was married to and how they wanted to exercise as much discretion as possible, they were not asked to attend the meeting. They informed John that they will make their decision within the next few weeks and that someone will deliver the Sunday sermons until they get back to him.

The day had come when the board would give its decision. The rumors alone had tarnished the church's name, and financial contributions had dwindled significantly. Given who the other party was, there was pressure to ensure John didn't preach in the community ever again. Even though there wasn't any concrete evidence to support this 'affair', John had been dismissed from his duties and asked to leave the church.

John felt shamed and hurt, even though he had done nothing wrong. He knew that they needed to move, start somewhere fresh. Somewhere where they wouldn't be reminded of this incident.

Sara was distraught. Next year would be her senior year; all she had ever known was Gunnison, Colorado, and all her friends were there, and she excelled at softball so much so that scouts were looking at her for college scholarships. She fought the idea of moving at first, but it wasn't until Steve, the Talsburt's son, started name-calling and bullying Sara that her decision changed. At first, it was just at school, and others would chime in, but then it escalated to vandalizing their home. After that incident, Sara was in complete agreement with leaving. Seeing how quickly people turned on her hurt.

Four days before their departure, Elaine went to the store to buy cleaning products to clean out their home. One of the benefits of being a pastor was the ability to stay in the parsonage. So, given that John was no longer the Pastor, they had to move out. Elaine, hurt but not wanting to make the situation worse, was determined to do a deep cleaning of the home. She was walking to her car, reading the label on a product she had purchased, when she bumped into none other than Mrs. Talsburt.

Elaine wanted to give in to the overwhelming rage that she felt come over her and yell, 'How could you lie? How could you destroy our lives with your foolishness?' But instead she froze, not sure what to say. She immediately thought, 'For we wrestle not against flesh and blood but principalities and wickedness in high places, ' she forced a straight face and continued to walk. As she passed by, she felt a hand grab her shoulder.

"Elaine, wait?" Mrs. Talsburt objected. "Would you please look at me?"

Elaine struggled to turn and face her. She said a silent prayer and looked in her direction, but not in her eyes.

"I want to apologize. I'm not even sure how this even got started, but know that the Pastor and I never had an affair."

"I know my husband, and I know he wouldn't do such a thing.

But what I don't understand is how this rumor started, or better yet, why you did not publicly say something?"

Mrs. Talsburt began to sob, and Elaine, unmoved by her gesture, started to walk away.

"Hold on!" fixing her face, "I never had an affair with anyone. My husband has been having an affair for years, and he even had a child with his mistress. He thinks I don't know, but I've known about it for some time. He has a two-year-old son, and he pays his mistress monthly. I thought that counseling would make it better. The last time I came to the pastor, I wanted to get advice on how to confront him. I was tired of his secrets and of the guilt I carried for silently condoning his behavior. When he heard the rumor, he didn't even get angry. I was hoping he would confront me, and I would call him out on his affair, but he didn't. When the church called to ask me about the affair, I denied it, but he took the phone and walked into another room. I couldn't hear all that was said, but I did get the gist that he wanted your husband gone. When he came back into the room, he told me to keep my mouth shut and do as he said. That I've caused enough embarrassment for this family. He's going to make a public statement tomorrow, and I'm sure that this is just another opportunity to shape his image in the press's eyes. I know him like a book, a book I am tired of reading. He's going to say he's forgiven me and how much he values family, blah, blah, blah. I'm so sorry, Elaine. I've perhaps said too much, but I'm truly sorry." And walked away.

And just like Mrs. Talsburt claimed, the mayor made a public statement stating he forgave his wife for her infidelity and how he believed in the family unit. Right after making that statement, he announced a new campaign initiative focused on families and said he had the backing of the very church that released John.

On the very day they were leaving, the headline reads, "Double Life: Mayor Promotes Family Values While Hiding Affair and Child."

* * *

Georgia, a place Sara's never been, yet held so much history for her. All she's known was the coldness of Colorado, but her mother and father were born and raised in Georgia. It was ministry that led them out of state.

It was a three-day drive to Georgia. Sara's mom wasn't much for driving, especially since they were in a rented truck with their van attached, so Sara's daddy did all the driving. After about ten hours of driving, they would find the nearest motel to sleep for the night. Sara hated sharing a room with her parents. Even though she would get her own bed, the annoying sounds of her father snoring sounded as if he were blowing a whistle every two seconds.

On top of that, she wasn't sure if it was menopause related or not, but her mother kept the room freezing. Sara was used to Colorado's weather outside, but she didn't enjoy the cold inside her home. She spent every night freezing and stuffing toilet paper in her ears in hopes of muffling the whistling.

Her parents would wake up feeling refreshed, while she was miserable. After the first night, she slept the entire car ride and stayed up for the remaining nights. She was so glad when they reached Georgia. She looked forward to having her own bed and not feeling like she was sleeping outdoors in Antarctica.

When they arrived, she found out they were going to live in a city called Stone Mountain, about twenty minutes from the capital, Atlanta. They arrived at a split-level house with beautiful pink and red Azaleas surrounding the mailbox and walkway. It was a slightly charming cottage home. Perhaps one of the nicest homes that they've lived in, well, at least from what Sara could tell from the outside. Sara's mom said that the pictures she saw made her pick the home. Plus, the rent was reasonably priced.

As they were parking in the driveway, there was a gentleman already at the front door. Sara guessed by the gentleman's grey hairs that he was slightly older than Sara's father.

"That must be Mr. Harrison," said Elaine as she waved from

inside the car. "He's the gentleman that we're renting this home from."

They all got out, and Mr. Harrison greeted them. He shook John's hands and nodded hello to Elaine.

Sara is not addressed, which is perfectly fine with her as her eyes wander around the neighborhood and eventually to the place she would stay.

Mr. Harrison offered to give them a tour of the place. "Sara, I figured this room would be perfect for you. It has a built-in bookcase and decent closet space," Elaine said, interrupting Sara's thoughts.

"Yes, Mom, I like it." Sara remained in the room as her parents and Mr. Harrison finished the tour. After a while, she could hear her father talking to Mr. Harrison about the rent before they signed off on the agreement. Shortly after, Sara could hear a car reverse out of the driveway, then her dad calling her name to help unload the U-Haul.

It was a long day unloading all their things. Elaine was tired and told John that she was going to rest for the evening. About twenty minutes later, Sara told her dad that she needed to rest, too. John continued for about an hour before he called it quits.

That night, because they hadn't set up any beds, the air mattresses were the next best thing. Sleeping on that air mattress was the best sleep Sara had had in days. She was grateful that she didn't have to deal with her father's snoring or her mother's—assumed—hot flashes.

After some days, they were able to get all the major items unpacked and in their rightful places. In some weeks, after rearranging a few things around the house and adding a few touches, they've managed to make it feel like their own. Well, as much as possible. It didn't feel like home to Sara, but then again, what would? They left 'home' because the people they trusted and thought cared for them turned their backs on them. What else was she to do but make the best of a messy situation?

Elaine had informed Sara that school would begin soon and that it was one of the best schools in the area. Elaine tried to encourage Sara and make her feel better, but it didn't seem to work. Most days, Elaine would catch Sara staring out of the window; occasionally, she would find her and John in the backyard playing catch.

Sara had mixed feelings about the first day of school. She understood the idea of adjusting to becoming a senior, but she also had to adapt to another school, in another state, with people she didn't know. She was starting all over.

The first day of school had arrived, and Sara found herself being dropped off in a carpool with other students, their parents ready to rid their homes of their children so they could do only God knows what. Sara never wondered what her mom did at home when they were in Colorado until the one time her mom was sick and stayed home from school. Her mom cleaned, cooked, hosted the other women from the church, and then took food to the sick and shut-in. But what would she do now that Daddy wasn't preaching and they weren't in Colorado anymore? Sara realized that this was an adjustment period for everyone.

Sara's homeroom class teacher was Mrs. Tuggle. She was a sweet yet stern middle-aged lady who demanded respect. One kid thought that it was okay to talk while she called roll. Mrs. Tuggle took out a yardstick and slapped it against the chalkboard to grab everyone's attention.

"I thank you all for being respectful and quiet while I call roll," she emphasized 'all' as she stared down the young man and went back to calling names.

Mrs. Tuggle gave them all their schedules, and after morning announcements, they were released to go to their first-period class. What should have been a thirty-second transition turned into four minutes. As soon as the bell rang, the hallway became crowded with students as if they were gnats fighting to get to fruit. By the time Sara reached the doorway into the hallway, she saw an opening straight ahead, so she made a dash for it. Rushing straight ahead may have saved her from being that girl who fell in the midst of the crowd, but it sent her in the wrong direction. After asking some teachers standing in the hallway to assist, Sara realized that her first period was next door to her homeroom.

Coach Daniels, an older man, was her first-period teacher. He was the English teacher and the basketball coach, hence the name Coach Daniels. He seemed very laid back for the first day of school, as if he'd done this several times, and his routine had become autopilot, but he'd rather be home. He gave them their class syllabus and told them they were expected to write in journals at the beginning of each class, so make sure they add a journal to the list of things to get by next week.

Sara was nervous about the idea of journaling. *Would he require us to read them aloud? Would he take them home and read them himself?* Were thoughts that marched in her head. The instructions were not clear to her, and based on his demeanor, she didn't care to ask for clarification.

The remaining first half of Sara's day seemed like a blur to her. She was late to all her classes because she wasn't used to the crowds. Gunnison, Colorado, was a small town where everyone knew each other, and the student-to-teacher ratio was eight to one. Her current school was more like twenty-five to one. Many more students flooded the hallways than she was used to.

Sara was grateful that her teacher, Ms. Lively, was understanding of her tardiness. And apparently, Ms. Lively was the only teacher who was kind enough to acknowledge that Sara was a transfer student and welcome her during roll call. She even encouraged Sara to get up and tell the others about herself. Sara honestly did not want to do so, as she was nervous, but she did not want to seem rude or make the wrong impression on her first day.

Another bell rang, and considering all the hassle Sara had experienced earlier, she decided to ask Ms. Lively for assistance. Looking at her schedule, lunch was next. Sara had no idea where the lunch hall was. Ms. Lively informed Sara to make a right out of her class. Make a left and go up the stairway. Make a right, another left, and the cafeteria will be on her right.

Sara tried her best to remember all of that after putting her books in her locker, but she may have taken a left when she should have gone right and ended up tripping over someone. She came crashing down in embarrassment, as her knees hit the ground and the back of her head grazed some lockers. Sara was thankful that she was still managing her pattern of being late, because if this had happened a few minutes earlier, she would have heard a hallway full of laughter and made a name for herself that would have haunted her the rest of the school year.

"You okay?" a voice said. Sara couldn't see the voice as her hair was covering her face and her shame as well. The voice repeated itself, and this time, she answered.

"Yeah, yeah. I'm alright, but my leg may not be," Sara managed to hobble up as the voice pulled her up with one hand. She stood up straight, and the pressure on her leg made her limp.

Not having made eye contact, the voice grabbed her shoulder and said, "You need me to take you to the nurse's office?"

She looked up and right into his brown eyes. "No, I'm okay," she mustered to say as she hopped again. The voice bent down and picked up her purse from the ground, seeing that she was struggling.

Handing Sara her purse, he asked, "You sure you don't want to go to the nurse's office?"

She stared for an uncomfortable amount of time, and when she realized that she had made this awkward moment worse, she managed to stutter, "Ye, yes, thank you though." Fixing herself, Sara began to explain, "I'm new and lost. I was looking for the cafeteria and..."

Another voice captured his attention, "Lewis, man, come on, we're going to be late."

Breaking Sara's focus, she turned to look behind her, and there he was, broad shoulders, hazel eyes, walking so confidently down the hallway. Perhaps it was his letterman's jacket or the way he tossed the basketball in the air, not missing a beat, that captured Sara's attention and left her standing with her mouth wide open, forgetting what she was saying.

"Come on man. What'cha doing?" he asked, with a certain twang.

"I'm coming, I'm just going to help?" Lewis lingered as he looked at Sara, waiting for her to fill in the blank.

"Oh! Sara. My name is Sara," she remembered.

"Yeah, I'm going to help Sara, and I'll be there, alright," Lewis assured him.

"Aiight, man, don't be late. I don't want to hear Coach's mouth."

"I got you," Lewis said to the other voice.

"I'm fine. I assure you. I don't want you to be late and your coach to be mad. My leg feels better." I convinced him.

"Alright. Well, Sara, right?"

"Yes, Sara."

"Take it easy, okay. The cafeteria is that way. Just keep going down the hall and you'll see it on your left.

"Thanks."

"Hopefully, I run into you again but not like this, okay?" he belted as he sprinted away to catch up with the guys.

Sara was at a loss for words, and all she could muster was, "Okay." While her morning had been going crappy, running into Lewis was an unexpected gift for her. Lewis had an almond-complexion face, and Sara thought he had beautiful eyes, but the icing on the cake was his voice. Sara thought his voice was fit for the radio, the kind you would listen to at night to soothe you to sleep.

Sara managed to find the cafeteria and stomach the bland ol' sloppy joe that they churned out. Sara's mom didn't have time to go to the grocery store before school started, so she gave Sara money to eat at school. Prayerfully, this would be the first and last time, Sara wished. She stomached what she could and studied her schedule before the bell rang to go to the next period. She looked around, heard laughter, and people catching up. It was like a family reunion. She could see a few stragglers, like herself, throughout the cafeteria. Sitting alone, contemplating life's choices.

Not too long after, the bell rang, and she was off to the races—trying to navigate the hallways and the rest of her day, but the stresses of the day were overcast by thoughts of Lewis's friend.

Chapter Two

Sara hurried down the crowded hallway, her eyes scanning the sea of students rushing to their next class. It had been a week since she'd last seen Lewis or his friend. She couldn't help but wonder if she would run into them again, but the whirlwind of schoolwork, softball practice, and trying to find her place at this new school kept her mind occupied most of the time. Still, she couldn't deny that a small part of her was always on the lookout for him, especially during lunch when she navigated through the bustling cafeteria.

Ms. Lively's classroom was at the end of the hall, and Sara quickened her pace to make it to her seat before the bell rang. Though Ms. Lively was sweet and approachable, she was also a no-nonsense teacher who expected her students to stay on top of their work. It was only the third week of school, and Ms. Lively had already assigned a major science project to be completed in groups. Sara had been teamed up with two classmates—Mark, a laid-back guy who didn't seem too concerned about anything, let alone schoolwork, and Ashley, a bubbly and well-liked girl who everyone seemed to know.

Ashley was the type of person who could light up a room with her smile. She had an easygoing charm, but Sara had noticed that she could be sharp-tongued when someone rubbed her the wrong way. Sara couldn't decide whether to befriend Ashley or keep her distance. As the only transfer student in the class, Sara often felt like an outsider, watching from the sidelines as everyone else navigated friendships that had been formed long before she arrived.

The science project was assigned in a way unfamiliar to Sara. She was used to picking her own teammates. Ms. Lively had them randomly draw from a box, with each student choosing a slip of paper with a topic written on it. When Sara pulled out her slip, she saw the words "Renewable Energy" scrawled across it. Mark groaned, clearly disappointed, while Ashley shrugged, as if she was ready to tackle whatever was thrown her way. They didn't have much of a choice, so the three of them huddled together in class to brainstorm ideas.

"So, renewable energy," Mark said, as he flipped his hair out of his eyes. "I guess we could do something with solar panels or whatever."

Ashley rolled her eyes. "We need to do more than that if we want to get a decent grade. Ms. Lively isn't going to be impressed with just a basic presentation."

Sara nodded in agreement. "What if we compared different types of renewable energy and analyzed which one would be most effective for our area? We could look at solar, wind, and maybe even hydro-electric power."

Mark sighed. "Sounds like a lot of work."

"It's a big project," Ashley said pointedly. "We should start planning now so we're not cramming at the last minute."

They discussed their ideas for a while longer, jotting down notes and setting tentative dates to meet up and work on the project. The deadline was approaching soon, and with homework and an exam scheduled for the week before, they knew they had their work cut out for them.

When the final bell rang, signaling the end of the school day, Sara gathered her things and made her way to the softball field. She had made the varsity team, which wasn't an impressive feat for her considering her experience. Back home, she had been one of the best players on her team, and she had hoped to continue that success here. But being the new girl on varsity had its challenges. Some of the other girls on the team seemed threatened by her, throwing her side-eye glances as if she were there to take their spot.

Despite the cold shoulders, Sara remained focused. She knew she was good enough to be on this team, and she was determined to prove it. As she jogged out to her position on the field, she reminded herself of her goals. She wanted to play softball in college and knew it meant giving her best effort every day, both on the field and in the classroom. Her parents had always stressed the importance of getting good grades. "You never know what could happen," her mother would say. "An injury could end your softball career, and you need to have something to fall back on."

Practice started well, with the team running drills and practicing their fielding. Sara was in her element, focused and determined to show her teammates that she deserved to be there. But then, out of the corner of her eye, she saw a group of boys jogging around the track that surrounded the field. Among them was Lewis, whose familiar face caught her attention. Her heart skipped a beat when she noticed that handsome guy she had seen Lewis with before, jogging beside him. There was something about him that drew her in, something in the way he carried himself that made her want to know more.

She was so distracted by the sight of him that she missed an easy fly ball. It soared over her head, landing with a thud on the grass behind her. The coach blew the whistle, and Sara's face flushed with embarrassment as her teammates groaned.

"Come on, Sara, that was an easy one!" one of the girls shouted.

Sara muttered an apology as the coach called her over. "That's five laps, Sara. You know better than to lose focus out there."

She nodded, knowing she deserved it, and started jogging around the field. As she ran, she couldn't stop thinking about the guy she had seen with Lewis. *What was his name? Would he even notice someone like her?* Her thoughts spiraled as she completed her laps, and by the time she finished, her legs were burning, and her mind was racing with questions she didn't have answers to.

When she rejoined the team, she could feel some of the girls watching her, their eyes narrowed with suspicion. She ignored them, vowing to stay focused for the rest of practice. She couldn't afford any more mistakes. She needed to prove that she belonged on the team, that she was just as good as anyone else.

After practice, one of her teammates approached her as they walked off the field. "Hey, don't worry about that fly ball," Nichole said with a smile. "We all make mistakes. Just try to stay focused out there, okay?"

Sara nodded, grateful for Nichole's kindness. "Thanks, I will."

Nichole glanced over her shoulder at the boys' basketball team, who were now walking towards the gym. "I saw you checking out the basketball team," she said with a grin. "Just be careful, okay.

The captain of their team is talking to one of the girls on our team, and you don't want to get caught up in any drama."

Sara's heart sank at the thought. The last thing she needed was to get involved in some high school drama. "Thanks for the heads up," she said, forcing a smile.

Nichole shrugged. "No problem. See you tomorrow."

As Sara headed back to the locker room, she couldn't shake the feeling of unease that had settled in her chest. High school was hard enough without adding complicated relationships into the mix. She didn't even know the guy's name, and already she felt like she was getting in over her head.

Chapter Three

Sara was exhausted from softball practice and the constant pressure of trying to prove herself both on and off the field. As she walked out to the parking lot, she spotted her mother's car idling near the curb. Sara sighed, mentally preparing for the "fun-filled" conversation that awaited her as soon as she slid into the passenger seat.

"Hi, honey! How was your day?" her mom asked, voice cheerful as always.

"Fine, mom," Sara replied, buckling her seatbelt and sinking into the seat.

"Just fine?" her mother pressed, glancing over at her with a smile that was both encouraging and expectant.

"Yeah, just fine," Sara said, knowing there was no avoiding what was coming next.

"Well, I've got some news!" Elaine said, shifting gears as they pulled out of the parking lot. "We're going to visit your Aunt Cynthia and Aunt Catherine this weekend! Isn't that exciting? You'll finally get to meet some of your cousins."

Sara tried to muster some enthusiasm but found herself focusing instead on the lingering thoughts of Lewis and his mysterious friend. The idea of meeting her cousins didn't hold nearly as much appeal as the possibility of running into Lewis's friend again. But Sara knew better than to voice those thoughts out loud.

"Sure, mom," Sara replied, her tone neutral.

"Oh, come on, Sara! You've heard so much about them! Aunt Cynthia and Aunt Catherine are looking forward to seeing you. You know, Aunt Cat is always asking about you. And Aunt Cynthia— well, she's just proud to have another niece to show off to her friends."

Sara knew all about her mom's two sisters. Aunt Catherine, or "Auntie Cat" as her mom liked to call her, was the youngest of the three siblings and, according to her mother, the wildest. 'A firecracker,' her mom would say, usually followed by some anecdote about how Aunt Cat had never been one to hold back her opinions, even when she probably should have. Sara had never met her in person, but she knew Aunt Cat had been divorced for a while and filled her time with whatever and whoever caught her interest.

Then there was Aunt Cynthia, the middle sister, who was the epitome of pride in motherhood. She had four children and was the first in the family to get pregnant, something she never let anyone forget. Sara had heard countless stories about how smart Aunt Cynthia was, how she had excelled in school, graduated with honors, and even completed a year of college before marrying Uncle Charles. Uncle Charles was now a judge —the same judge who had made a few well-placed phone calls to get Sara into the private school she attended, the kind of school typically reserved for the wealthy or well-connected.

"Did you hear what I said, Sara?" her mom asked, breaking through her thoughts.

"Yeah, I heard you," Sara said, snapping back to the present. "We're visiting Aunt Cynthia and Aunt Catherine this weekend."

"That's right," her mom said, nodding approvingly. "It'll be good for you to spend some time with them. Family is important, you know."

"I know, Mom."

"Besides, you'll finally get to meet your cousins. I know they are some years older than you, but I bet you'll all get along great!"

Sara didn't share her mother's optimism. The idea of spending the weekend with cousins she'd never met, nearly a decade older than her, and aunts who seemed more like characters in a family saga than real people, filled her with a sense of dread. But she kept those feelings to herself. There was no point in arguing with her mom about it.

As they drove home, her mom kept up a steady stream of chatter, recounting stories about Aunt Cynthia's latest achievements and Aunt Catherine's most recent adventures. Sara nodded along, half-listening as her mind wandered back to school, to the mysterious boy she had seen with Lewis. She wondered if she would see him again, if he even knew she existed. The thought made her heart race a little faster.

Before Sara knew it, they were pulling into the driveway. Her mom parked the car and turned to her with a smile. "Why don't you start packing tonight? We'll leave early Saturday morning so we can spend the whole day with your aunts."

"Okay, mom," Sara said, grabbing her backpack and heading inside.

Once she was in her room, she flopped onto her bed and stared at the ceiling. The weekend was looming, and with it, the pressure to make a good impression on a family she barely knew. But as much as she tried to focus on that, her thoughts kept drifting back to Lewis's friend. She couldn't shake the feeling that she had to know more about him.

Saturday morning arrived much sooner than Sara would have liked. Her mom was up bright and early, buzzing around the house as she made sure everything was packed and ready for their trip. Sara dragged herself out of bed and went through the motions of getting ready, all the while wishing she could stay home and avoid the whole ordeal.

By the time they hit the road, Sara's mom was already in full storytelling mode, recounting every detail she could remember about her sisters. Sara listened with divided attention, nodding at the appropriate moments of her mom's stories, while her thoughts were miles away.

"So, Sara, are you excited to meet your cousins?" her mom asked, breaking into her daydream.

"Uh, yeah, sure," Sara replied, not entirely convincing. Sara's dad looked at her through the rearview mirror and gave her a warning look to mind her tone.

Elaine, unaware of Sara's disinterest, continued, "You know, your cousin James studied business, just like your Uncle Charles wanted him to. I'm sure he'll have lots of advice for you about getting into a good college."

Sara couldn't help but roll her eyes at the thought. 'Advice' from someone who doesn't know her and who was ten years older wasn't exactly high on her list of priorities.

"And then there's Emily," her mom continued, "you two should have a lot in common. She loved softball when she was your age. Maybe she can show you around town while we're there."

"Great," Sara said, trying to sound enthusiastic to please her dad. The last thing she needed was to be paraded around town by a cousin she didn't know.

As they pulled up to Aunt Cynthia's house, Sara's mom took a deep breath. "Here we are! Now, remember to be on your best behavior, okay? Aunt Cynthia is very particular about manners."

"Got it, mom," Sara said, opening the car door and stepping out.

Aunt Cynthia's house was exactly what Sara had expected—large, well-kept, and a bit intimidating. The front yard was perfectly manicured, with neatly trimmed bushes and a row of colorful flowers lining the walkway. Sara couldn't help but feel a little out of place as she followed her mom up to the front door.

The door swung open before they could even knock, and there stood Aunt Cynthia, a slender woman with perfectly styled hair and a warm, albeit slightly rehearsed, smile. "Sara, it's so good to meet you finally!" Aunt Cynthia exclaimed, pulling her into a tight hug.

"Hi, Aunt Cynthia," Sara said, her voice muffled against her aunt's shoulder.

"My, you've grown into such a lovely young lady," Aunt Cynthia said, stepping back to take a good look at her. "Come inside, all of you. The rest of the family is just dying to meet you." Sara had never met any of her family. Her mom and dad moved to Colorado from Georgia before she was born. Even when Sara was old enough, she would hear her mom on the phone, talking to her sisters. Sara would even give the casual 'hi, hello' now and again, but nothing of substance. Sara asked why they never go to visit, and her mom would always give some roundabout excuse tied to her father's schedule and having so much to do. Sara knew it was something deeper, but she avoided it, just like her mom.

Sara followed her mom into the house, her stomach tightening with nerves. As they walked through the entryway, she could hear voices coming from the living room: her cousins, no doubt.

"There they are!" Aunt Cynthia announced as they entered the room.

Sara looked around, trying to take it all in. Sitting on the couch were her two cousins, James, a serious-looking guy who was clearly the oldest, and Emily, a pretty girl with a friendly smile. Standing by the fireplace was Uncle Charles, who gave Sara a nod of approval.

"Sara, this is James and Emily," Aunt Cynthia said, gesturing to the two on the couch.

"Hi," Sara said, feeling awkward under their scrutiny.

"Hey, nice to meet you," James said, offering a polite smile.

"Hi, Sara! I've heard so much about you!" Emily added, her smile warm and genuine.

"Nice to meet you, too," Sara replied, relaxing a little.

"And of course, Uncle Charles," Aunt Cynthia said, turning to her husband.

"Hello, Sara. Welcome to our home," Uncle Charles said, his voice deep and commanding.

"Thank you, Uncle Charles," Sara said, trying to sound confident.

"Why don't we all sit down and get to know each other better?" Aunt Cynthia suggested, motioning to the chairs around the room.

Sara took a seat next to her mom, who was already in conversation with Aunt Cynthia about the latest family news. Sara did her best to pay attention, but her mind kept wandering. She couldn't help but feel like an outsider in this polished, picture-perfect family.

"So, Sara, how are you liking your new school?" James asked, breaking her train of thought.

"It's okay, I guess," Sara replied, not sure how much to share.

"Just okay?" Uncle Charles pressed, his brow furrowing slightly.

Sara hesitated, then remembered that her mom said that Uncle Charles had made some phone calls to get her into this school. "It's a good school. It's just—different from what I'm used to," hoping she had said the right words.

"I can imagine," Emily chimed in. "That school can be pretty intense."

"Yeah, it is," Sara admitted, glad to have someone who seemed to understand.

"Well, if you ever need any advice, just let me know," James said, offering a reassuring smile.

"Thanks," Sara said.

Chapter Four

Sara wasn't exactly excited about this weekend's visit at first. But as it turned out, her time with Aunt Cat was surprisingly enjoyable. Aunt Cat, as Sara quickly learned, was an absolute hoot. The woman had a way of making everyone around her laugh, and she was so laid-back that it was hard not to relax in her company. Sara found herself feeling more at ease than she had in weeks.

"I'm telling you, Sara," Aunt Cat said with a grin as she poured herself another glass of iced tea, "high school might be tough, but you've got to enjoy it. I still go to the games sometimes, even though my kids are all graduated and grown. Keeps me young, you know."

Sara laughed. "You mean you go because of that 'friend' who teaches there, right?"

Aunt Cat winked, "Well, that too. But don't go telling your mom now. She'll think I'm trying to relive my glory days."

The weekend went by faster than Sara had expected, and soon enough, she found herself back at school, trying to get through with their science project. Despite their best intentions, her group had yet to meet up. Between Sara's softball practice and Ashley's cheerleading, they barely had time to breathe, let alone work on their project.

Mark, the only one who didn't play sports, had been complaining during one of their brief meetings. "I don't see why we're stressing over this," he said, leaning back in his chair. "Female sports don't even get that much attention anyway."

Sara rolled her eyes, but then an idea struck her. "Actually, Mark, that might be the solution to our problem."

Mark looked confused, "What do you mean?"

"Well, instead of trying to find time outside of what we're already doing, why don't we use that time to work on our project?" Sara suggested. "Ashley and you could come to my softball practice, and we could use that as the backdrop for our project on kinetic energy—converting physical sports movements into a practical example of energy transfer. In return, Mark and I could attend Ashley's practice and analyze the cheer routines biomechanically. We could provide insights on how to enhance movements for better stability and performance."

Ashley's eyes lit up. "That could actually work! I'd just need to run it by my coach since our practices are sometimes closed."

Mark didn't seem to mind, probably because it meant he'd be around girls and get to see cheerleaders up close. "I'm in," he said with a shrug.

Sara nodded, satisfied with their plan. They had two weeks to implement it, so there was no time to waste. The first practice they attended, the boys' basketball team was also practicing in the gym. The cheerleaders practiced on the stage, while the basketball players ran laps on the floor. As Sara listened to the cheerleaders, she couldn't help but notice one of the players.

Ashley's practice had ended, and Sara couldn't help but ask, "Who's that?" She whispered to Ashley, nodding towards a tall, athletic-looking guy who seemed to be leading the team.

Ashley glanced over. "Oh, that's David. He's the captain of the basketball team."

Sara couldn't take her eyes off him. There was something about the way he moved, the way he seemed to command everyone's attention in the room, that kept her captivated.

Ashley nudged her. "Someone's crushing, I see."

Sara blushed. "Me? No, I'm just admiring from afar."

"Sure," Ashley said with a smirk. "But you should know, all the girls are into him. He's focused on the game, though. Wants to go pro one day."

Sara's heart sank a little. "You like him too?"

Ashley shook her head. "David? No way. He's like a brother to me. We started at this school the same time. And as you can see, there aren't too many of 'us' here, no offense. Everyone wanted us to get together, but it's never been like that between us. David has dated a few girls here, nothing serious. He likes to keep his options open, if you know what I mean."

"Oh," Sara said quietly, trying to hide her disappointment.

"Just don't get your hopes up," Ashley added as they left the gym.

Sara nodded, but as they exited, she glanced back and saw Lewis waving at her. She smiled and waved back, her heart lifting a little. Maybe there was still hope.

That night, Ashley's words echoed in Sara's mind. "Don't get your hopes up," she had said. But no matter how hard Sara tried, she couldn't get David out of her head. She recited a verse to herself-"Take every thought captive to the obedience of God"-repeating it over and over until she fell asleep.

The following week was a challenge. Sara found it difficult to focus on anything other than when she might see David again. Between her own practices and Ashley's, she only made it to the gym once, and neither of the guys was there. The week before their project was due, Sara suggested they all stay after school one day to make sure everything was in place.

Everyone agreed, and after their rehearsal session, Sara took the long way to the carpool section, hoping to catch a glimpse of David. She had told her mom to pick her up later than usual, buying herself some extra time.

As she waited outside, the boys' practice ended, and there he was —David. He looked like a breath of fresh air, even though he was sweaty and clearly exhausted. As he walked towards the parking lot, Sara's heart raced.

"Sara?" a voice interrupted her thoughts.

She turned to see Lewis approaching. "Hey, Lewis. And yes, you remembered correctly," she said, trying to hide her excitement.

Lewis smiled. "You alright? I don't usually see you here this late."

"Waiting on my mom. We had to work on a science project after practice," Sara explained.

"Ms. Lively's class, right?" Lewis asked.

"Yeah, how did you know?"

"Ashley mentioned it to us; she said you were pretty smart about getting things done."

"Us?" Sara asked, raising an eyebrow.

Lewis nodded towards the parking lot where David was standing. "David and I. Ashley's like our sister. We look out for each other."

"That's sweet. How long have you all been friends?" Sara asked, genuinely curious.

"Ashley and I since middle school, and David and I since ninth grade. You're new here, right?"

"Yeah, moved here from Colorado."

"Colorado? Wow. Don't think I've ever met anyone from Colorado." Lewis paused for a brief moment, building up the courage to say, "So, do you think I could take you out sometime? Show you around." Lewis asked, his tone casual but hopeful.

Sara hesitated. "I'd like that, but I don't think my father would approve."

"I understand," Lewis said, his smile fading a little.

"But if anything changes, I'll let you know," Sara added quickly.

"Alright, I'll see you later then," Lewis said, waving as he walked away.

Sara watched him go, her heart fluttering with uncertainty. David was waiting by the car, and she couldn't help but wonder if she'd done the right thing by turning Lewis down. Maybe she could go out, but just not on a date.

Her mom arrived and carried her away, but the thought lingered in her mind as she made her way home. She knew her dad wouldn't be okay with her going on a date, so she came up with a plan. The next day at school, she approached Ashley with an idea.

"Ashley, do you think you could come over in a few days to study? My parents are a bit overprotective, and I think they'd feel more comfortable if they met you before I asked to hang out over the weekend," Sara explained.

Ashley grinned. "Of course! I'd love to meet your parents."

When the day came, Ashley came over for dinner. The atmosphere was a bit tense, with Sara's dad keeping a close eye on her friend, asking probing questions. Sara learned that Ashley's father and mother divorced when she was in middle school, but now it's just her and her mother. Her father moved out of state. Sara's mom nudged her father, genuinely happy that Sara was making friends and didn't want him to scare her away.

After dinner, with her mom's encouragement, Sara took the opportunity to ask. "Mom, Dad, do you think I could hang out with Ashley this Saturday?"

Her mom gave her dad a look, the kind that said, 'Come on, let her have some fun. 'Her dad hesitated but finally nodded. "Alright, as long as you're home by five."

"Five?" Sara blurted out. "Can I stay until eight?"

Her dad sighed but eventually agreed. "Okay, eight, but no later."

"Thanks, Dad!" Sara said, giving him a quick hug.

Ashley, who had been watching the exchange, chuckled as they headed back to Sara's room. "Your dad is tough, huh?"

"You have no idea," Sara replied with a smile.

With her parents' green light, Sara told Ashley to set up a time with Lewis and David for the weekend. When Saturday came, the four of them met up, and it turned out to be a great time. Lewis spent most of the day walking Sara around the city, pointing out different places while Ashley and David stayed behind.

At one point, Sara found herself shoulder to shoulder with David. There was a moment of silence, a spark of something unspoken, but then it passed. As the day ended, Sara couldn't help but feel a mix of emotions—happiness, confusion, and maybe a bit of longing.

As they all said their goodbyes, Lewis smiled at Sara. "Today was fun. Maybe we can do it again sometime?"

"I would love to," she tried to suppress her Chester cat-like smile. If it weren't for her nearly losing her balance, she would have sworn she was walking on clouds.

It was something she liked about Lewis, yet she was drawn more toward David. Perhaps it was his confidence, his personality, or the mystery of him. Sara's never been with anyone outside of her race. Honestly, Sara's never been with any boy before. Her father wouldn't allow her to date. Back home in Colorado, everyone knew each other and knew Pastor John's rules pertaining to Sara.

Chapter Five

Sara was able to slow down a little after completing the science project with Ashley and Mark. It was one less thing she had to stress about. And Sara discovered why she rarely saw Lewis during the school day: their classes were on opposite sides of the campus.

Lewis started showing up to watch her softball games before heading to his own basketball practices. Softball was going exceptionally well, and Sara was at the top of her game. The team had made it into the finals. The championship game was scheduled a week before homecoming, and Ashley encouraged Sara to run for Ms. Softball on the homecoming court since she was running for Queen.

"I think you'd be perfect for Ms. Softball," Ashley said one afternoon as they worked on Ashley's campaign posters.

Sara was hesitant. "But I don't have time to really focus on it. The championship game is all I can think about."

Ashley smiled. "Don't worry, I've got you. I'll help with the campaign stuff. I know how it is when the team needs you to focus. Trust me."

Sara nodded, grateful for the support. With Ashley taking charge of most of the campaign, Sara could concentrate on the upcoming game. Her mom was excited, not just about the championship but also about her running for the homecoming court. She was excited about her friendship with Ashley because it was getting Sara outside her comfort zone. Her dad, on the other hand, was a little hesitant and advised her not to get caught up with people's opinions, and to remember that beauty is vain. Sara understood her dad's heart motive, but it was starting to be a buzz kill for her.

The day of the championship game arrived, and the excitement was palpable. The stands were filled with cheering fans, including Sara's parents, Aunt Cat, most of her cousins, and even her grandparents. Everyone was there to support her.

The game was intense. With two players on base and the team down by one, Sara found herself at bat. The pressure was overwhelming, but she steeled herself, focusing on the pitcher. The first pitch was a strike, the second a ball, but the third— the third she sent soaring over the fence for a home run.

The crowd erupted as her team surged ahead by two. Now, all they had to do was keep the other team from scoring. And they did. The victory was theirs, and Sara was named the game's MVP. Her face was all over the school newspaper that week, and for the first time, she felt like she truly belonged. Her teammates' respect was the cherry on top.

The following week, Sara was voted Ms. Softball during homecoming. Her parents were thrilled, and they even allowed her to stay for the rest of the homecoming game as long as Aunt Cat kept an eye on her and brought her home.

Aunt Cat, always the cool and laid-back one, gave Sara a bit more freedom. "Just meet me back here at the end of the game. Have fun," she said with a wink.

Sara sat near the cheerleaders to support Ashley, who was crowned homecoming queen. Some of Sara's teammates joined her, and they spent the game laughing and celebrating their recent victories.

After the game, Ashley bounced over to Sara with a grin. "A

bunch of people are heading to the diner to celebrate. Lewis and David will be there. You coming?"

Sara hesitated, but before she could say anything, Ashley added, "Come on, I'll make sure Aunt Cat is cool with it."

Sure enough, Aunt Cat agreed, even offering to cover for Sara by telling her parents she was spending the night at her place. "Just be back by midnight," she warned.

All four of them, Sara, Ashley, Lewis, and David, rode to the diner in Lewis's car. On the way there, Sara sat in the front seat with Lewis, chatting about the game and how excited she was for the night. But when they arrived at the diner, David pulled a surprising move.

"Hey, Sara, why don't you sit over here?" David suggested, patting the seat beside him.

Sara felt a flutter in her chest as she nodded and took the seat. Throughout the meal, David was attentive, asking her about the game, her campaign for Ms. Softball, and getting to know her more. Lewis could tell that David had captivated her attention because not for a moment did Sara look away from David. Lewis tried to hold himself together and not express his disappointment. Lewis was used to David getting all the girls; that's what he does. But Sara was different. Sara was his interest.

When the bill came, David insisted on paying for her meal, congratulating her again on the MVP win. Lewis, being the gentleman he is, opened the car door for Sara, assuming she would sit up front with him on the ride back, but David insisted again that Sara sit with him. She blushed and opened her own door to the back seat.

Lewis' heart sank a little more, but in a smooth motion, he looked at Ashley, smiled, and gestured that the front seat was hers for the taking. He closed the door, ensuring that Ashley was safely in. As he walked around the side, he eyed the two in the back, silently wishing that it was he and Sara. As he shook the feeling, his heart became hardened.

Lewis dropped Sara off first to make sure she got to her aunts on time. David walked her to the door, a gentlemanly gesture that didn't go unnoticed.

"I had a really good night," David said, his voice warm and sincere.

Sara smiled up at him, feeling her cheeks heat up. "Me too. Thanks for everything."

David smirked, placed his hand on her shoulder, and said, "Anytime, MVP."

Sara melted in that very moment. With that, he gave her a small wave and headed back to Lewis's car, leaving Sara standing at her front door, heart pounding with excitement.

The following week, Sara was in Coach's class working on the writing assignment when David knocked on the door. Coach looked up from his desk, surprised to see him. "David, what's up?"

David walked over, saying something to the coach that Sara couldn't quite hear. But she noticed that, while talking, he glanced over in her direction and gave her a wink. Sara felt her face flush again. After finishing his conversation with the coach, David made his way over to Sara's desk. "Hey, Sara, I was wondering if—"

"David, back to class," Coach interrupted, his voice firm but amused.

David gave a mock salute, grinning as he backed away. "I'll see you later, Sara."

Sara watched him leave, her mind racing. Now that David knew where her class was, she saw him more often. He made it a point to walk down her hallway between classes, always stopping to chat for a moment or two.

"You should come watch us play sometime," David suggested one day as they walked together between classes.

Sara couldn't hide her excitement. "I'd love to. I'll have to ask my parents, but I'm sure they'll let me." Sara wasn't sure. In fact, she dreaded asking her parents, but she had to make this work. She was determined to find a way. It was David. Her David.

When she told Ashley about it later, they giggled together like schoolchildren. "Oh my gosh, I think he's totally into you!" Ashley teased.

"Stop it," Sara said, though she couldn't stop smiling and hoping it was true.

Ashley and Sara had grown closer, bonding over everything from school projects to their shared victories in sports and homecoming. They had become almost inseparable, always there to support each other, whether it was during practice or in the stands, cheering each other on.

One day after school, Sara was walking toward the parking lot when she saw David heading in the same direction. Her heart skipped a beat as she quickened her pace to catch up with him.

"Hey, David," she called out.

He turned, smiling when he saw her. "Hey, Sara. Heading home?"

"Yeah, my mom's picking me up. You?"

"Just finished practice. You know, you should really come to our game tomorrow. We're up against our biggest rivals, and I could use some extra support," David said, his tone teasing but hopeful.

Sara grinned. "I wouldn't miss it for the world."

They walked together for a few more minutes, chatting about their classes and upcoming games. When they reached the parking lot, David paused.

"By the way, I was wondering if you'd like to go," hesitant to ask, "with me to see a movie?" David's eyes meet hers.

Sara's heart leaped in her chest, causing her to blink from staring into David's eyes, "I'd love to."

David smiled, clearly pleased with her answer. "Great. I'll see you at the game then."

As Sara watched David walk away, she couldn't help but feel that things were finally falling into place. She had aced her project, won the championship, been crowned Ms. Softball, and now she had a date with David for the movies; life couldn't get better than this.

The next day, Sara worked it out and attended David's basketball game, sitting with Ashley and some of their other friends. The gym was packed, and the energy was electric. David was in his element on the court, leading his team with skill and determination. Every time he made a shot, the crowd roared, and Sara found herself cheering louder than anyone.

During halftime, David caught her eye from across the gym and gave her a small wave. Sara waved back, feeling her cheeks warm under his gaze.

"You've got it bad, girl," Ashley teased, nudging her playfully.

Sara laughed, unable to deny it. "I guess I do."

After the game, which David's team won, he found Sara in the crowd. "So, what did you think? Not bad, huh?" David asked with a confident grin on his face.

"You were amazing," Sara said, genuinely impressed.

"Thanks. I'm glad you were here. It means a lot." David said as he smiled and headed back to the locker room.

Sara waited around with Ashley, talking with friends, recapping the game, laughing, and enjoying themselves. David and Lewis came out from the locker room, laughing and roughhousing with each other. As they all met up and walked out of the gym together, David asked Sara if she wanted to grab a quick bite to eat with him and some of the other players. With Aunt Cat covering for her, she agreed.

They ended up at a local pizza place, where the team celebrated their victory. David made sure to sit next to Sara, and they spent the evening laughing, talking, and enjoying each other's company. It felt natural, easy—like they had been this way forever.

Chapter Six

Sara had always been determined, but it wasn't until the past few months that her life had begun to shift in ways she hadn't antici- pated. After the success of her softball team, the subtle, growing connection with David, and the increasing bond with Ashley, she felt herself transitioning from a high schooler focused solely on grades and sports to someone on the brink of adulthood, navigating friend- ships, relationships, and family expectations.

Sara finally convinced Ashley to come to church with her family. Sara had always wanted to share her world with Ashley, and with the strength of her friendship, this seemed like the perfect opportunity.

The morning was crisp, the sky a bright blue, and as they walked into the church, Ashley's discomfort was palpable. "You know, I've never been to a white church before," Ashley whispered as they took their seats.

Sara smiled, trying to ease the tension. "Nothing to worry about. No one's going to notice."

They chuckled, but Ashley's eyes wandered nervously around the sanctuary. As the service progressed, Ashley remained quiet, absorbing the experience. The music was different for Ashley. While Ashley hadn't been to church in years, she remembered going to church with her grandmother as a child. She would be amazed at the liveliness of everyone during the praise and worship. The shouting mothers during the sermon. She would have some good laughs at the older mothers of the church, unaware of what was going on but appreciative of being able to watch.

Afterward, as they walked out, Ashley admitted, "It wasn't bad. Good message. Quiet, but I did appreciate how short it was." Ashley returned to Sara's home for an early dinner after service and spent the rest of the day talking with Sara in her room before it was time for her to leave.

As the weeks passed, Sara became a regular at David's games. Sitting with the cheerleaders, she found herself not just watching the games but becoming friends with the girls she once viewed from afar. David made sure to wave at her as he entered the court, and every game she attended, he seemed to play with a bit more energy. It was becoming their unspoken ritual—she was there for him, and he noticed.

One day, during a visit to Aunt Cat's house, Sara confided in her about wanting to attend an away game. "My parents won't let me go," she sighed, frustrated. "Especially Dad. He's all about safety and control."

Aunt Cat, never one to let her niece down, winked at her. "Well, I think you'll be spending the weekend with me, and when you do, maybe we'll go out to a high school basketball game and enjoy ourselves."

The weekend arrived, and Aunt Cat, true to her word, took Sara to the game. It was a crucial match, and anticipation was thick in the arena. People were ready to boil over at the start of the game. Aunt Cat sat a few rows away, giving Sara space while keeping a watchful eye. During a timeout, Sara noticed Aunt Cat giving Coach Daniels a playful wink. Her eyes widened in realization. *Is she involved with Coach Daniels, my English teacher?*

Despite her surprise, Sara focused on the game. David and Lewis were on fire, leading their team to victory. As the final buzzer sounded, signaling their win by twelve points, the crowd erupted in cheers. Aunt Cat came down from the bleachers, grinning. "I'll see you at home by midnight. Have fun!"

Instead of the usual diner hangout, this time the celebration was at Lewis's house. Sara had no idea what to expect, but as they pulled up, she was taken aback by the size of the place. The driveway alone looked like it could fit a dozen cars. Lewis, ever the gentleman, opened the door for her. "Welcome to Casa de Lewis," he joked as they walked inside.

The party was in full swing in the lower half of the house. His parents greeted them briefly before heading upstairs. They gave the partygoers a stern but kind reminder: "No drugs, no alcohol. We'll be upstairs if you need anything."

Sara was impressed by the house. Everything from the grand staircase to the luxurious furnishings spoke of wealth. "Your home is beautiful," she remarked to Lewis.

"Thanks," he replied, leading her to a quieter corner. Sara couldn't help but notice how every girl at the party seemed to have her eyes on David. David moved effortlessly from one conversation to another, always surrounded by admirers. "My parents are both lawyers. They have their own practice." Lewis continued, causing Sara to refocus.

"Do you plan to follow in their footsteps?" Sara asked, genuinely curious.

Lewis shook his head. "No, I'm more into engineering. But they're cool with it."

Lewis was enjoying this alone time with Sara. Getting to talk to her and learn more about her and her world. As he was forgetting he was the host of the party, a commotion broke out near the pool table. "I need to handle that," Lewis said, sighing as he went to break up the argument.

Sara sat alone for a moment, still taking in the house's grandeur.

A boy she vaguely recognized from school approached her and struck up a conversation about the softball championship. They had barely started talking when David appeared, his presence commanding immediate attention.

"Hey, man," David said, his voice casual but firm. "Someone's looking for you." Quickly catching on, the boy made his exit, leaving Sara and David alone.

Sara, always the one to make light of situations, teased him, "Looks like you're making your rounds. Just needed to cross me off your list?"

David laughed, his eyes locking onto hers. "Nah. Those other girls were keeping me from getting to the one person I actually want to spend time with."

Sara blushed, feeling the sincerity in his words. It was like they were in their own little bubble, oblivious to the world around them. "Let's find somewhere quieter," David suggested.

Sara hesitated, her eyes scanning the room. "I'm fine here, with everyone else. I wouldn't want anyone to get the wrong idea or for your admirers to get jealous."

David grinned. "I get it. But just so you know, I like that you're different from all the other girls."

Feeling a surge of confidence, Sara allowed herself to be pulled into a dance. "Fair warning," she joked, "White girls don't dance like this," pointing to everyone else who was dancing.

His lips curled into a playful smirk, guiding her to the makeshift dance floor. "Don't worry, I got you."

At first, Sara felt self-conscious, trying to match the unfamiliar rhythm of the music. But with David cheering her on and Ashley hyping her up from the sidelines, she let go of her insecurities. The night was filled with laughter, the kind that made her stomach ache and her heart soar.

As the night wore on, Sara knew she had to leave to make it back to Aunt Cat's by midnight. Lewis, the epitome of a knight in shining armor, walked her upstairs. He introduced her to his parents, who were warm and welcoming, asking her about her interests and plans for the future. Lewis, sensing her discomfort, quickly intervened. "We need to go. Don't want her to break curfew."

His parents nodded, reminding him to drive safely and return straight home. Outside, the night air was cool, and Sara shivered slightly. Lewis noticed and immediately draped his jacket over her shoulders. "You cold?"

"A little," she admitted, grateful for the warmth.

They walked to the car, and their hands brushed against each other. Lewis turned on the heat and placed his hand next to hers. "Did you have a good time?" he asked, his voice soft.

Sara smiled, their fingers lightly touching. "I did. It was nice to meet your parents, too."

The drive back to Aunt Cat's was filled with comfortable silence, a testament to the growing bond between them. When they arrived, Lewis walked her to the door, ensuring she was safely inside before heading back to the party.

* * *

Time passed, and the excitement of prom began to buzz through the school. Sara was thrilled when her parents finally agreed to let her go, though under the strict condition that she wouldn't have a date. On the night of prom, while her friends arrived in a limo, Sara's mom dropped her off at the venue.

She met up with Ashley, and they met some other girls at the prom. Some had dates and others didn't, which made Sara feel better about her situation. After Sara's experience at the party, she allowed herself to be free to dance without so much concern for others.

Joy twinkled in Sara's eyes when David danced with her. She jokingly asked, "Where's your date?" knowing that if he actually had one, she would be heartbroken.

But David, captivated by her, responded that, even though she couldn't have a date for prom, he wanted to make sure he spent his time with her.

His response had Sara feeling like a princess. Like the whole night and everything else were set up for her, for them. For Sara, time at prom was a vapor; it vanished in the blink of an eye, but in those three hours, her fairytale had come true. But as the clock struck eleven, her mom was outside waiting for her. Having to walk away, Sara felt a pang of sadness. She was grateful for the moment, but it was hard for her to let it end.

The next day, she spent the afternoon with Ashley, eager to hear all about what happened after she left. They lounged in Ashley's room, surrounded by snacks and photos from the night before. "So, what did I miss?" Sara asked, trying to keep her tone light but her heart to hear everything about David.

Ashley filled her in on the details, including how Lewis had disappeared for a bit but returned before the night ended. "You know, everyone was talking about how David barely danced with anyone else after you left," Ashley teased, nudging her friend.

Sara blushed, feeling a flutter of happiness. "Really?"

"Really. I think he's feeling you," Ashley said with a wink.

They spent the rest of the day talking about college and the future. Both Sara and Ashley, along with David, had been accepted to the same in-state university, hours away from home. They were excited but also a little nervous about the changes ahead. Lewis, on the other hand, had applied out of state, pursuing his dream of becoming an engineer.

Graduation day arrived, a bittersweet moment filled with excitement and nostalgia. As Sara walked across the stage to receive her diploma, she glanced out into the audience. Her parents, aunts, and cousins were all there, cheering her on. But it was David's gaze she sought, finding comfort in his familiar, encouraging smile.

After the ceremony, they all gathered outside, taking pictures and sharing stories. Sara couldn't help but feel a mix of emotions: pride for all she had accomplished, but also a sense of loss as this chapter of her life came to a close.

As they stood in the parking lot, David came up beside her, slipping his hand into hers without being seen, "Ready for the next adventure?"

Sara squeezed his hand, and a smile spread across her lips.

Chapter Seven

Sara stood in the middle of her dorm room, surrounded by half-unpacked boxes, feeling a mix of excitement and anxiety. Her parents were busy helping her get settled, but the reality of starting college was sinking in. Her father, the concerned parent, kept reminding her to stay focused on her studies, while her mother fussed over the smallest details, like making sure her bedspread was perfectly aligned.

Before they left, her father suggested they all hold hands and say a prayer. As they circled up in the small dorm room, her mother squeezed her hand tightly, and Sara felt a pang of homesickness. They prayed for her success, safety, and guidance during her freshman year. Sara nodded along, trying to ignore the lump in her throat. After a few minutes, her parents hugged her one last time and left, leaving her alone in her new room.

The dorm was designed for four students, each with their own small room. Sara was slightly disappointed that she wasn't able to get the same dorm as Ashley, who was staying two floors below her. David was in a different building altogether, but Sara figured she would see him around campus.

Days into her freshman year, Ashley was serious about convincing Sara to go to a party on campus. "Come on, Sara! You've got to experience college life! We can stay out all night, no curfew, no parents. It's our first taste of freedom!" Ashley was persistent, and despite her reservations, Sara eventually agreed. The party was at a frat house within walking distance from their dorm.

When they arrived, the house was packed with students, music blaring from every corner. Sara scanned the room, hoping to spot David, but didn't see him. She tried to relax and enjoy the party, but a part of her felt out of place. The atmosphere was different, unsettling. It wasn't until she finally saw David that her mood took a turn for the worse. He was standing across the room, laughing and flirting with another girl. A surge of jealousy and sadness welled up inside her, but she tried to push it down.

"Come on, let's dance!" Ashley pulled Sara towards the dance floor, but Sara's heart wasn't in it. She managed to dance for a few minutes before retreating to a couch in the corner. Ashley stayed on the dance floor, lost in the music, while Sara sat alone, in her feelings.

Not long after, a guy approached her. "Hey, I noticed you were sitting here alone. Thought you might need a drink and some company," he said, handing her a red cup. "I promise, I didn't do anything to it." His expression softened into a warm, inviting smile.

Sara hesitated for a moment but then thanked him and took a sip. The guy introduced himself, and they started chatting. He was friendly and seemed genuinely interested in her. Sara took a few more sips, feeling a bit more relaxed. However, about fifteen minutes later, she started to feel "off." Her head felt heavy, and her vision was slightly blurry. She felt weak, and before she knew it, she was leaning against the guy for support.

"Are you okay?" he asked, concern lacing his voice.

"I, I don't feel so good," Sara mumbled.

"Come on, let me take you home," he offered, helping her to her feet. Sara nodded, too disoriented to argue. As he guided her towards the stairs, Sara's legs felt like jelly beneath her. Just as they were about to head upstairs, David appeared out of nowhere.

"Where do you think you're going?" David demanded, stepping in front of them.

The guy holding Sara scowled, "Back off, man. She's fine. I'm just helping her out."

David's eyes narrowed, his posture tense. "I don't think so. Let her go."

The guy sneered, clearly annoyed, but after a moment of tense silence, he relented. "Whatever, dude. She's all yours." He practically shoved Sara into David's arms before storming off.

David wrapped an arm around Sara's waist to steady her. "Come on, let's get you out of here."

Sara woke up the next morning with a pounding headache, a dry mouth, and an aching body. She blinked against the bright light filtering in through the window, trying to piece together what had happened the night before. Slowly, she realized she wasn't in her dorm room. Panic surged through her until she noticed David sleeping on the floor beside the bed.

She let out a small sigh of relief but still felt a gnawing sense of unease. What happened? Why were they in the same room?

David stirred, hearing her move. He opened his eyes and sat up, his expression unreadable.

"David, what happened last night?" Sara asked, her voice shaky. She was afraid of the answer but knew she needed to know.

David's expression softened. He could sense what she was worried about and quickly reassured her, "Nothing happened, Sara. I promise. You were pretty out of it, so I brought you back here to make sure you were safe. I slept on the floor."

Sara's face flushed with embarrassment and a bit of shame. "I, I don't remember much. I was talking to some guy, having a drink, and then everything went blurry."

"Did you make the drink yourself, or did he bring it to you?" David asked, his tone serious.

"He brought it to me. He seemed nice," Sara replied, her voice small.

David sighed, shaking his head slightly. "Sara, you've got to be more careful. Don't ever take a drink from someone you don't know, especially a guy at a party. He probably put something in it and was planning to take advantage of you. I stopped him before he could do anything."

Sara's eyes widened in horror. "Before he could...I... I didn't even think about that. Why would someone even—"

"You're going to have to learn quickly," David said gently. "You're not in high school anymore or a small town. There are people out here who don't care about you, who won't think twice about hurting you. Did you go to the party with Ashley?"

"Yeah, but she wanted to dance, and I didn't, so I stayed on the couch," Sara admitted.

David sighed again, more heavily this time. "I'll talk to Ashley, but you two need to stick together. That's girl code. Why am I the one having to teach you this?"

Sara felt a twinge of defensiveness, "Teach me?"

"Yeah, Sara. You didn't have a sister or any girlfriends who taught you this stuff back home?"

Sara looked away, a lump forming in her throat. "I don't have a sister. My twin died at birth. And I grew up in a small town in Colorado. You know how my father is, so going out wasn't an option for me. Plus, I moved to Georgia before my senior year, so I didn't really have any close friends, except for you all."

David's expression softened with understanding and a slight hint of regret for his question. "So you didn't have any friends back home who talked about this stuff with you?"

"I had friends, but considering my dad was the town's preacher, everyone respected me, I guess. I never missed a curfew, and I didn't feel like I missed out on things. My friends would come over for sleepovers, and we never had to worry about a 'girl code,'" she air quoted.

"I get it," David said, nodding. "But you've got to stay on your toes here. Your daddy's reputation isn't going to save you out here."

Sara felt a mix of shame and relief. Shame that she had been so naive, but relief that David had been there to protect her from something worse happening. "Thank you, David," she said softly.

David gave her a small smile. "Anytime."

After that night, Sara vowed she wouldn't go to any more parties. She saw firsthand how quickly things could go wrong. She focused on establishing a routine with her classes, which were scattered across campus. For a couple of weeks, she struggled to make it to her back-to-back classes on time. Thankfully, one of her professors was lenient about attendance, but Sara wanted to make a good impression and started pushing herself to arrive early.

As the weeks went by, Sara found her rhythm. She packed snacks and a lunch to avoid the long trek back to her dorm between classes. Some weeknights, Ashley would come over to Sara's dorm to eat together. While Ashley wasn't particularly fond of cooking, Sara found it relaxing. Ashley would often joke that Sara's cooking was good but needed a bit more seasoning. While Ashley wasn't much of a cook, she knew what good food tasted like and was glad to help Sara sharpen her skills.

Ashley and Sara shared the same math class. David had the same professor but attended on different days. After a few exams, Sara was averaging an A, Ashley a B, and David a C. He needed to raise his grade to stay on the basketball team.

One day, Ashley ran into David on campus, and they caught up. When David mentioned his struggle in math, Ashley immediately thought of Sara. "You should ask Sara to tutor you," she suggested. "She's acing the class, and she explains things in a way that makes sense."

David agreed, pleased at the idea of time with Sara. With this transition to college, it hadn't been an easy adjustment as he thought it would be. The first tutoring session was at Sara's dorm one evening while she was cooking dinner. Ashley was there, and the three of them chatted as Sara worked in the kitchen. David was impressed by her cooking, and Ashley joked about how she had to teach Sara a thing or two about seasoning.

As the tutoring sessions continued, Ashley wasn't always able to attend due to her other commitments. One night, it was just Sara and David in her dorm room, going over equations and working through the math problems. They'd been at it for a while, and the night had grown late. Sara leaned over the textbook, trying to explain a particularly tricky concept to David, who was leaning in close, his focus on her every word.

"Does that make sense?" Sara asked, glancing up at him.

David didn't respond immediately. His eyes lingered on her face, and for a moment, Sara felt her breath catch. There was something in his gaze, an intensity that hadn't been there before. The air between them shifted, the math forgotten.

"Sara." David's voice was soft, almost hesitant.

Before she could think, he leaned in and kissed her. It was gentle at first, almost as if he was testing the waters, but it quickly deepened as Sara responded. The world seemed to tilt, and for a few blissful seconds, everything else faded away.

But then reality crashed back down on her. Sara pulled back, her heart racing. "David, we can't."

David looked as if he'd been jolted back to reality, too. "I'm sorry, Sara. I didn't mean to—"

"No, it's not that," Sara interrupted, her voice shaky. "I just. I don't want anything to happen that we'll regret." Fumbling with what to do or say, she forcefully voiced, "It's late, and you should go."

David nodded, looking a bit crestfallen. "You're right. I'm sorry, I didn't mean to make you uncomfortable."

David gathered his things, and Sara walked him to the door. There was an awkwardness between them now, a tension that hadn't been there before. As he left, Sara leaned against the door, her mind swirling with confusion and guilt.

She liked David. She'd liked him for a long time, but what she felt when they kissed, she'd never felt before. It was as if something had pulled her in. An overwhelming wave of emotions that she wasn't sure if she should fight against or allow to consume her. Before she walked into her room, she whispered, "Trust in the Lord with all your heart and lean not on your own understanding; in all your ways submit to him, and he will make your paths straight." She kept repeating, "In all your ways submit to him." She repeated it all night long until she drifted away into the slumber of the night.

The next day, David didn't show up for their usual study session. Sara waited, hoping he would come, but as time passed, it became clear that he wasn't going to. She tried to focus on her own studies, but her mind kept drifting back to the kiss—to the way David had looked at her. To the way she had felt.

But was she the only one he had done that with? That was what scared her. She realized that, with him not coming, she was better off. She couldn't face him, not now. She assumed he had learned enough to get a passing grade in the class and decided to let things be for now.

Chapter Eight

It was near the holiday break, and you could sense the anxiety on campus. Some moved around like ghosts, pale and haunted by the weight of the exams, knowing their parents would kill them if they flunked out. While some sparked with nervous energy, ready to prove themselves.

"So, Lewis and I thought we should all meet up at the local diner when we go home for break, to catch up," Ashley chuckled, ricocheting around all the stuff spread out on Sara's floor. Then she added, "Who's in?"

Sara nodded absently, "That makes sense."

"Yeah, he spoke to me about it," David added as calmly as possible.

Ashley's smile faltered. "What's up with you two?"

The room went quiet, and the buzz of their collective sighs thickened the air.

"It's nothing," Sara said, too quickly. She pretended to be busy. But it was something. She had been avoiding David like a pop quiz on a subject she had never studied before. She would only catch glimpses of him on campus, always rushing off to one class or another to avoid contact.

And today, when she saw him leaving the math building with another girl, her heart felt like it was being squeezed by a vice, quickly convincing her that the 'kiss' wasn't a special moment between the two. That indeed he had done it before with others.

"You guys are the worst at hiding it," Ashley said, leaning in. "Spill."

"It's just—finals," Sara murmured, trying to sound nonchalant. "We're all stressed."

Ashley snorted. "Since when does David stress about exams? Plus, we're done. There's nothing you can do about it now. So, are y'all going to tell me what's up with you two?"

The question hung there, unanswered. Sara felt the weight of Ashley's stare, but she couldn't bring herself to explain the hollowness that had settled in her chest. How could she put into words that she was jealous of seeing the guy she had sent out after he kissed her, with another girl, and that her heart had bloomed like a toxic flower at the sight of David with someone else?

"Fine," Ashley said, standing up. "You can wallow in your own sadness. But I'm going to live it up before we head home. Who's coming to the party tonight?"

"It's been back-to-back studying and exams, wouldn't you rest at least?" Sara asked her ever-bubbly friend.

"What other way is there to unwind than dancing and meeting a few cute guys?" Ashley replied, determined to enjoy herself and not let Sara and David's issue bring her down.

Sara watched as her friends exchanged glances. "I'll stay in," she said reluctantly, "I've got a lot of packing to do."

Ashley studied her for a moment before nodding. "Okay, but if you change your mind."

The door clicked shut behind them, leaving Sara alone with her thoughts. She had to admit, the distractions from her thoughts did seem tempting. But the thought of seeing David, especially in the midst of a celebration, was too much to bear. Not to mention, the idea of something similar to her first college party experience was enough to shut it down.

As she lay on her bed, the walls closed in around her, and she heard the distant chatter of students passing by. A strange ache grew within her, one that she couldn't quite name. *Was it just the sting of regret or something deeper?*

Her emotions for David were a puzzle in pieces that she wasn't sure fit. It was like she had a glimpse into who he was, and what she saw reflected him as a lady's man, and that kiss definitely meant nothing to him. But it did a lot for her. She didn't want to be led astray, but with her emotions in an uproar, she realized it was too late for that.

She heard a knock, and her bedroom door creaked open, and she sat up, hope flaring in her chest. But it was her roommate. She wanted to borrow something. Sara felt the hope fizzle out like a deflating balloon.

Sara sighed, staring at her phone. She'd told Ashley she didn't want to go, but the loneliness was real. Her thumb hovered over David's name, but she couldn't bring herself to text him. Not after she'd seen him with that other girl.

Sara spent her time cleaning up her room and packing. Having glanced at the top of her desk, she noticed her Bible that had lain there. She stopped what she had been doing, sat there, and looked at it for a moment.

Her mind wandered to the hours before, when he and Ashley were in her room. The way he'd looked at her before he left was like he was saying goodbye, but not just for the break. And now, alone in her room, left with the taunting of her imagination, she felt an unease growing inside her.

She didn't like the feeling, so she prayed and flicked open her Bible. She began reading passages about God's mercy, forgiveness, and His love. It started to chip away at the hardness of her heart and unravel the twisted bundle of her emotions.

She was engulfed in reading for some time when her bedroom door was forcefully opened. Startled, she jumped, her cheeks flushed and eyes bright, but relief came as she recognized it was Ashley,

"You're not going to believe this," Ashley said, breathless.

Sara's heart pounded. "What?" anxiously anticipating that something bad had happened, explaining the abruptness of Ashley coming into her room.

"I saw David with another girl!" While it wasn't the type of news she expected, it was bad enough.

The words hung in the air, hurting Sara as if salt was being rubbed in her wound. She swallowed hard, trying to keep the tears at bay. While Sara had already seen him with a girl earlier, she wondered, if it was the same girl. Or was it someone different? Trying to play clueless, "What do you mean?"

Ashley flopped down on the bed, a mix of excitement and concern etched on her face. "He was leaving for a party with the guys, and he was with this girl. So, doing me, you know, I had to intervene and ask. He said she's his new tutor. But they looked," Ashley paused, seeing Sara's face and unsure if she should say it, "close."

Sara heard what she said but didn't comprehend, "She is who?"

"His new tutor," Ashley said, her voice dropping to a whisper. "But she's pretty, and they were laughing together, and his arm was around her neck. I just thought you should know. Y'all have been acting funny, so I'm not sure if y'all are 'together' or not, but.."

Cutting her off, not wanting any more details, "Thanks," Sara, forcing it out.

Her friend leaned in, her eyes searching. "Come on! Are you guys okay? Do you need me to go and mess her up or something? I know you're too good to lay a hand on someone, so I can go to the party and trip her up, spill a drink on her, or something. Just give me the word."

"No, don't do that. We're good," Not knowing what else to say, she lied. All these feelings were new to her—overwhelming and suppressing how the thought boiled inside of her to give David a piece of mind and to show 'that' girl that David was off limits.

Ashley squeezed her hand. "Well, if you change your mind."

Sara nodded again, the motion mechanical. After Ashley left, Sara stared at the wall, her thoughts racing. She had to get out of here. The walls were closing in, suffocating her with memories of David's laughter, his gentleness with her, his easy companionship. The ache in her chest grew sharper with every beat of her heart.

That kiss had opened a Pandora's box of emotions that she's never felt before. With a deep breath, she grabbed her coat and headed out into the cool night air. The wind bit at her cheeks, but it felt good, cleansing. She walked aimlessly, the distant sounds of a party fading into the background. The quiet was calming, but it only amplified her thoughts.

Why was he with someone else? Did he not care about her anymore? Or had she been fooling herself all along? Maybe he never even liked her, but then why did he kiss her? A lot of unanswered questions at once.

Her feet carried her to the library, a place where she felt a sense of calmness. She pushed open the heavy doors, the scent of old books and stale coffee enveloping her. It was almost empty, the only sound the occasional rustle of pages and the hum of the heating system.

As she wandered through the library, her eyes fell on a book titled "The Art of Moving On." She couldn't help but laugh bitterly. It was as if God had placed it there, mocking her. But she picked it up anyway, needing something to distract her from the pain.

The book was filled with stories of people who'd faced rejection and heartache, only to find something better on the other side. Sara read until her eyes grew heavy, each tale resonating with her own feelings of loss.

When she finally looked up, time was far gone. She left the book on the table and made her way back to the dorm, feeling a little lighter. Maybe there was something to this moving-on business. She read a few scriptures and prayed. This offered her the peace she needed to close her eyes and pursue rest.

* * *

The music grew louder, the bass thumping in Ashley's chest, as she stepped in, ready for the night.

The party was in full swing when Ashley and her roommate, Jenna, arrived. The lights danced and flickered, casting shadows that played tag with the figures as they moved to the music's rhythm. The air had the scent of cheap beer and overpriced perfume. Ashley felt a mix of excitement and nerves as they pushed through the crowd. Jenna, on the other hand, was in her element. Her laughter bubbled like champagne as she greeted friends and flirted with strangers.

They spotted a group of guys across the room, leaning against the wall with the casual confidence of lions surveying their pride. Jenna's eyes lit up, and she tugged Ashley's arm. "Come on, let's go talk to them!" she shouted over the music. Ashley hesitated, but the promise of a good time and the buzz of the crowd propelled her forward.

As they approached, one of the guys looked up. His eyes locked onto Ashley's, and she felt a jolt of attraction. He had a crooked smile, yet he was attractive. His name was Jake, and he was as charming as he was disheveled. They talked and danced, the night stretching out before them like a winding road filled with laughter and the potential for romance.

The party grew louder, the music more insistent. Time passed in a blur of smiles and shared glances. The room was a kaleidoscope of colors, the lights pulsing in time with the beat. Ashley felt alive, her heart racing with every step she took closer to Jake. Jenna had paired off with one of his friends, leaving them to flirt unabated.

But the night had a darker side, a shadow that would soon creep into Ashley's world. As the party wound down and the guests began to filter out into the cool night air, she found herself alone with Jake. He offered to walk her back to the dorm, and she accepted, feeling a flutter of excitement in her stomach. She had no idea that the walk home would lead her down a path she never wanted to take.

The night was quiet, the moon a mere sliver in the sky. The street lamps cast a feeble glow, leaving the spaces between pockets of darkness. Jake's hand found hers, and she squeezed it, feeling comforted by his presence. But as they approached a secluded alley, something changed. His grip tightened, his smile grew predatory, and she realized with a sickening jolt that she had made a terrible mistake.

The alley was a cage, the walls of the surrounding buildings pressing in on her. She tried to pull away, but he was too strong. Panic surged through her as she felt his hands on her, violating her in a way she had never imagined. She screamed, but the music from nearby parties was too loud, the night too indifferent. No one came to her rescue.

When it was over, Jake disappeared into the night, leaving her alone with her pain and fear. She lay there, trembling and broken. The alley was cold, the rough concrete biting into her skin as she gathered herself together. She didn't know how long she stayed there, but eventually, she found the strength to stand.

Walking back to the dorm added to the nightmare. The pain she felt between her legs was incomparable to the pain she felt emotionally and mentally. Each step felt like a betrayal, her body screaming for her to run, to hide. It was as if shame was riding on her back and filth was talking in her ear, scoffing at her. Helplessness had covered her eyes as everything had become a blur, and she wasn't quite sure how she made it to her room.

Ashley was tucked in bed and had tucked the horror into a corner of her mind. Wrapped in blankets and layers of denial and numbness, it was a secret she would carry with her. A heavy burden that would shape her days and haunt her nights. It wasn't until Jeanna burst into her room to get the details of the night that she had closed her eyes. She pretended to be asleep in hopes that Jeanna would leave. Jeanna whispered her name twice, but when there was no response, she left.

That night, after Jenna went to bed, Ashley sat in the shower, the water scalding her skin, trying to wash away the memories. The tears fell in time with the droplets, mixing with the steam to form a sad, silent symphony. She didn't know how to go on, how to live with the weight of what had happened. The fear of someone finding out, the fear of being seen as damaged, was suffocating.

* * *

Sara stepped out of her dorm into the brisk morning air, the scent of freshly brewed coffee wafting from the café counter. The chirping of birds, and the distant rumble of students who were leaving with their luggage for the break.

She proceeded with one of her weekend routines, of grabbing a cup of coffee, strolling through campus, and sitting on her favorite bench to plan her day. It was a routine that brought her comfort, a sense of normalcy in a life that had grown increasingly tumultuous.

As she approached the café, the barista, a cheerful young man named Tim, greeted her with a smile. "The usual, Sara?" he asked, already starting on her order. She nodded, feeling the weight of unspoken words tugging at the corners of her mouth.

The warmth wrapped around her like a cozy blanket. She took a deep breath, inhaling the aroma of freshly baked muffins. Tim handed her the coffee, giving her a questioning look. She managed a smile, "Thanks, Tim. Just what I need." He nodded, his eyes lingering on her for a moment before he turned to serve the next customer.

The campus was quiet and almost empty as some people had already headed home for break. Her breath misted in the cool air. Sara found her bench and sat down, sipping her drink. She watched the sun peek over the horizon, its soft glow casting long shadows across the dewy grass. Her thoughts drifted to David, the guy who had become a central figure in her life, yet remained a puzzle she couldn't solve. His actions confused her, his intentions a blur.

Her heart was a tangled mess of emotions. Sara knew she needed to talk to Ashley about David. She needed to get this off her chest as it had been weighing on her. Sara had been drowning in sadness and the overwhelming sense of confusion.

She thought about the conversation that Ashley had with her when she saw David with another girl. She knew her heart wasn't in a good space when she envisioned hurting someone. She had repented, but she needed to expose those deeply buried thoughts.

Back home, she would talk to her mom about a lot of things, but never a guy. She never had to before. But she knew her mom would tell her dad, and that would be a chain reaction that would make the situation worse.

She took another sip of her coffee, the warmth spreading through her body, and stood up, ready to cast off this anchor that had her stuck.

Walking to Ashley's dorm, she rehearsed the words in her mind, trying to find the right balance between honesty and sensitivity. As she stepped onto Ashley's floor, the sound of her footsteps echoed in the empty hallway. The dorm door was unlocked, as was typical. She knocked softly on Ashley's room door.

"Come in," Ashley said, her voice devoid of its usual cheer. Sara stepped inside, noticing the dark circles under her friend's eyes, her disheveled hair, and the sadness that clung to the air like a thick fog.

She probably hasn't had a good night's rest, Sara thought. She sat down on the chair, set her coffee on the table, and took a deep breath. "I need to talk to you," she began, her voice trembling slightly. "It's about David."

Ashley's expression grew guarded, the sadness in her eyes momentarily replaced by a flicker of something Sara couldn't quite place. But before Ashley could say anything, the dam broke, and Sara's words spilled out in a rush. She talked about the moments that confused her, the little things that didn't add up, the kiss, and the fear that maybe she didn't know David as well as she thought she did. As she spoke, Ashley nodded along, her face a mask of understanding and empathy. But Sara couldn't shake the feeling that something was off.

Ashley remained silent, appearing to listen intently. When Sara finally paused to catch her breath, the room was heavy with unspoken secrets. Ashley took a deep, shaky breath and looked away, the silence stretching between them like a tightrope threatening to snap. "I know you're going through a lot, and thinking about so many things," Ashley finally said, her voice barely above a whisper. "But I can't... I just can't talk about it right now."

The frustration bubbled up in Sara's chest. Ashley had been asking her what was going on, and when Sara finally decides to confide in her, her response is 'She can't right now?'

"What's going on with you, Ashley? Have you even been listening? This is a huge problem for me, and it's eating me up! And that's what you tell me?" Her voice filled with frustration.

Ashley's eyes snapped back to hers, a flash of anger sparking in them. "You want to talk about problems?" she snapped; the words tinged with bitterness. "You have no idea what I'm dealing with!" The room felt suddenly too small, the air thick with accusation and pain.

Sara was about to continue to lash out when she looked up and realized Ashley's eyes were filling with tears; she hadn't realized they were there. "Is everything okay?" Sara sat back, stunned. She had no idea what had just happened. All she knew was that she was now as lost and confused about her friend as she was about David. "I'm sorry," she managed to say, her voice small. "I didn't mean to make it all about me. I just. I need your help."

Ashley's expression softened, the anger dissipating as quickly as it had come. She took a deep, shuddering breath. "Yeah, right," she said, her voice cracking. "Well, I'm sorry too. But I just. I can't right now, Sara. I can't."

"What's wrong, Ashley? Yesterday you were fine, and now—something is off? Will you please tell me what's going on?"

The two friends sat in silence, the weight of their unspoken words hanging in the air like a storm cloud. Sara felt a pang of guilt for unloading her burdens on Ashley when, unbeknownst to her, she was struggling with her own. But she also felt a growing sense of urgency about David. The conversation with Ashley had only made her more confused, and she didn't know what to do next.

Ashley never gave a response as she battled between giving into the overwhelming desire to be comforted, hoping that the filth that took place last night could be washed away, and the wall that was being built, knowing that what happened couldn't be undone, and no one would understand what she was going through.

Sara noticed Ashley was deep in her thoughts, so she stood up and gave Ashley a gentle hug. "I'm here for you," she said, "whenever you're ready to talk."

With a heavy heart, Sara left Ashley's dorm, pulling the door behind her with a finality that echoed through the hallway. As she walked back to her dorm, the rumbling sounds grew louder, drowning out the thoughts in her head. Her mind kept drifting back to David and the conversation she needed to have, but wouldn't.

As she finished her coffee, Sara made a decision. She would keep avoiding David as she had been doing. She wouldn't know what to say to him even if they were to meet. Would she tell him that she loved him and was scared he saw her as one of his lady friends? The possibility that David wasn't who she thought he was frightened her; the fear was overwhelming, but she knew she couldn't go on like this, living in a world of doubt and uncertainty.

Chapter Nine

Ashley lay in her bed, her blankets shielding her from the world. The sun casts a gentle glow through the curtains, but she was determined to ignore it. Her eyes remained shut, her breathing shallow. The room was silent except for the occasional creak of the floorboards, a stark contrast to the tumult inside her. Each breath she took felt like a battle against the weight of unspoken words and unshed tears.

Jenna knocked on Ashley's door but noticed it wasn't shut all the way, so she pried it slightly open as she had done so many times before.

"Hey, I'm packing up. You okay?" Jenna said and asked. Jenna noticed something off about Ashley and wondered why. Finals were over, and they were all about to go home for the break today. Ashley should be excited.

"Yeah, I'll be fine." The lie was as much for Jenna as it was for herself.

"Alright then, if you say so, "Jenna said as she left. Her footsteps grew faint as she went back to her room.

Ashley's phone buzzed. It was a message from her mom, and it read, "On my way. Be ready."

Ashley's heart raced at the thought of her mother's impending arrival. She had been submerged in her overwhelming emotions, so going home was far from her mind. Her mom had always been her nightmare, and school had always been her escape, but now even school felt like hell; she couldn't add her mother's shenanigans to the way she felt at the moment.

With trembling fingers, she typed out a response. "Don't worry, I'll ride back with Sara." The lie slipped out effortlessly. She heard the front door open and close as Jenna departed. The dorm felt eerily quiet once more.

The hours ticked by, the sun peeking through the gaps in the curtains. Ashley's stomach yelped, but she didn't move. Sara sent her a text to let her know she'll be leaving soon, and she wanted to come by to say bye before she left. Ashley dismissed her by saying she wasn't feeling well, and she didn't want to get her sick, and that she would catch up with her later.

It was true; she didn't lie. She felt sick to her core, a space where food couldn't fill the void, and she would see Sara—eventually. Her mind raced with thoughts of what people would think, what they would say. The fear of their judgment was a heavier burden than the truth she carried.

As the shadows grew longer, she finally sat up, the weight of her decision pressing down on her shoulders. Her eyes searched the room, landing on the rumpled clothes from the party. The fabric whispered of betrayal and pain. She couldn't face her friend's concern, her mother's wrath, or the cold stares of people when they found out what happened.

"You two are home early," Elaine called out from the kitchen, her voice a blend of surprise and warmth.

"Yeah, Dad was able to beat the rush," Sara replied, dropping her bag in the hallway. The smell of roasting chicken filled the house, a comforting scent that was as much a part of home as the creaky floorboards beneath her feet.

Her mom rushed around the corner, with a dish towel slung over her shoulder, and gave Sara the biggest hug she could muster up. "How was your trip?"

"It was okay," she said, her voice a little flatter than she had intended. She had been looking forward to this break, but the shadow of David still lingered, casting a gloom over her excitement.

In the living room, the Christmas tree twinkled with lights, reminding her of happier times. She felt a pang of longing for the days when the holidays were filled with laughter and love, rather than the echoes of her confused love story and her worry about her friend.

Sara slumped onto the couch, her eyes tracing the familiar patterns of the quilt that had been there since they moved to Georgia. Her thoughts were interrupted by the buzz of her phone. She took it out of her pocket, hoping it was at least a message from Ashley, but it was just a notification for a group chat she had with some classmates. With a sigh, she scrolled through her contacts, her thumb hovering over Ashley's name.

They hadn't talked since Ashley lashed out at her, but she needed someone to talk to, even if it was about the person's issues, anything to get David off her mind. Her heart racing as she dialed her number. It rang a few times, and just as she expected, she got no response.

She decided to go for a walk around town after convincing her father that she was mature enough to be on her own for a while, since she had managed to be on campus on her own. About fifteen minutes into her walk, she bumps into Lewis.

"OMG, hey Lewis!" His height made him stand out in the crowd, and his easy smile was like a beacon. They hugged briefly, and she felt a familiar comforting warmth, and that hug was a stark reminder of what he'd lost. "I would say that I am surprised to see you, but it is winter break. How are you?"

"I'm good. School's good, but I miss all of you! How's everything going with you?"

Sara continues with a fake smile and a story, but as quickly as the idea came to mind, it dissipated, and her tone changed. She spoke to him about all that bothered her, not knowing that Lewis had feelings for her, and she friend-zoned him. She kept talking about how she cared for David and how jealous she felt when she saw him with another girl. She tells him about Ashley, too, and how she had lashed out at her a few days ago.

"It's a tough situation, but you can't let this ruin your break. And about Ashley, we need to figure out what's going on. I haven't heard from her in a while, either.

Sara nodded. "I tried calling her, but she didn't answer."

"Well," Lewis said, his voice calm and steady, "we'll get to the bottom of this."

They brainstormed ideas on what could be the issue with Ashley, their conversation a mix of hope and concern. Sara decided she would pop over to Ashley's mom's house to check in on her, hoping she would open up. Sara knew Ashley didn't care to be with her mom for the holiday, so perhaps a nice walk around town would trigger the good memories they've shared and would be enough for Ashley to open up and tell Sara what's going on.

Sara arrived at Ashley's place, but unbeknownst to her, Ashley's mom told Sara that Ashley said she was riding home with her. So, she thought that she was staying at her place. She invited Sara in. It was now apparent that something was definitely wrong with Ashley. Her mom called Ashley's phone twice, but she didn't answer.

As she sent her a text asking why Sara was here looking for her if she claimed that she was riding home with her. She texted her mom back to say that she stayed on campus. She wasn't feeling well, so she didn't want everyone to get sick during the holidays.

"She says she's sick and doesn't want to put anyone at risk, so she stayed back. She's your friend. You should know about this without me telling you," Ashley's mom said, her breath reeking of alcohol.

Sara wondered what kind of mother would be this relaxed about her daughter not coming home for the holidays. She texted Ashley to ask if everything is truly okay because she realized she lied to her mom and is avoiding everyone. With this situation, coupled with her lashing out, she knew something serious had to be going on.

Sara's message read:

"Tell me if everything is okay. I would come back to campus to be with you if you wish. Please, just don't shut me out."

* * *

The streets were blanketed with a thick layer of fresh snow, the kind that crunched satisfyingly underfoot.

The day had come for them to meet up at the local diner—it was what Ashley had arranged with Lewis and would probably be their last time seeing Lewis until the next semester break.

David stood outside the small diner, its neon sign flickering "Open" against the cold December sky. He adjusted his scarf, breath puffing out in white clouds as he peered down the street. He pushed open the door —a bell jingled overhead —and the warmth of the diner welcomed him in.

Seated at a booth near the window, Lewis waved him over with a grin. The table was already adorned with two steaming mugs of hot chocolate, marshmallows bobbing at the surface.

"Hey, man," David greeted as he slid into the seat across from Lewis, shaking the snow off his coat. "Been a while."

Lewis smirked, taking a sip of his drink. "Yeah, too long. I almost forgot what you looked like."

David laughed, the stress of Sara's silence finally starting to melt away. "Tell me about it. So, how was your trip home? Everything cool with your family?"

"Yeah, everything's good," Lewis replied, his tone warm. "It was nice to see everyone. Just a lot of eating, a lot of talking, and you know, the usual 'what are you going to do with your life' kind of conversations."

David nodded, knowing all too well how that felt. "Yeah, tell me about it, my parents are the same, you know how my dad is, the old man can't go a day without asking what the plan is after graduation. I keep telling them I'm still a freshman, bro."

Lewis leaned back in his seat, stretching out his arms. "It's tough, man. But we'll get there. Anyway, I'm glad we could at least catch up tonight. I was hoping to see everyone, but I guess it's just us."

Lewis said, waving his phone across David's face. It was a text from Sara. He quickly read it, "Sorry, not going to make it."

He sighed and slipped his phone back into his pocket. "Yeah, Sara's not coming. And Ashley—well, Sara said, she decided to stay on campus, which is too bad. I was looking forward to seeing her, especially since we planned this together."

"Campus?" David asked, surprised.

"Yeah, Sara thinks something is wrong. I think so, too."

"Oh," David said, but there was a hint of something unspoken in his voice. He took a deep breath, pushing the thoughts away. "But it's all good. We'll all catch up eventually."

"Hopefully," Lewis agreed, though he noticed the slight tension in David's expression. "So, how are things with you and Sara? It's obvious she's not here because she's trying to avoid you."

David hesitated, staring into his hot chocolate as if it held the answers he was searching for. "I don't know, man. Things got complicated during finals. We haven't really talked much since then."

Lewis nodded slowly, not pressing further. He knew when to give space and when to offer a listening ear. Instead, he changed the subject, especially if the discussed subject was his love interest.

"So, any plans for New Year's?"

David smiled, grateful for the shift in conversation. "Not really. I'm thinking about just staying in, maybe watching the ball drop with the family. What about you?"

"Same here. My mom always insists on making this huge dinner, and we all end up watching movies until midnight. It's a tradition at this point," Lewis said, a fond smile on his face.

"Sounds nice," David said, genuinely envious of the simplicity. "Maybe I'll crash your place."

"You're always welcome," Lewis laughed, raising his mug in a mock toast.

As they talked, the snow outside continued to fall, covering the town in a serene, quiet blanket. The diner was nearly empty, except for an older couple at the counter and a waitress humming along to a Christmas tune playing softly over the speakers.

David found himself relaxing, the warmth of the diner and the comfort of Lewis's company easing the worries that had been gnawing at him since the semester ended. There was something about being home, surrounded by the familiar, that made the uncertainty of the future seem a little less daunting.

Meanwhile, across town, Sara sat curled up on the couch in her parents' living room, the Christmas tree twinkling with lights beside her. She was surrounded by her family, Auntie Cat, and her cousins, the room filled with laughter and holiday cheer. Her mother was in the kitchen, finishing up the last of the holiday cookies, while her father was deep in conversation about the latest football game.

Sara should have felt content, and on the surface, she did. There was something deeply comforting about being home, the familiarity of it all wrapping around her like a warm blanket. But despite the peace around her, a part of her mind was still elsewhere. David.

She couldn't stop thinking about him. She had told herself that the break would be a good time to get some distance, to sort through her feelings. But it seemed that the more she tried to push thoughts of him away, the more they came rushing back. She told herself she had to get it together because softball season was starting, and she needed to stay focused.

"Sara, honey, you okay?" Elaine's voice broke through her thoughts.

Sara looked up, startled, to see her mother standing before her, a plate of cookies in hand. "Oh, yeah, I'm fine," she replied with a forced smile. "Just thinking."

Her mother set the plate down on the coffee table and sat beside her. "You've been quiet tonight. Is everything alright? You seem a little," trying to find the right word, "distracted."

Sara hesitated, not sure how to put her feelings into words. "It's just school stuff," she said vaguely. "You know how it is."

Her mother nodded, though her eyes held a knowing look. "Well, if it gets too overwhelming, don't forget to pray, and if you ever want to talk, you know I'm here. The holidays are supposed to be a time to relax and enjoy, not worry."

"I know," Sara said, her voice softening. "Thanks, mom."

They sat in silence for a moment; the only sound was the crackling of the fire in the fireplace. Outside, the snow continued to fall, covering the world in a blanket of white. Sara watched the flakes drift down, each one unique and fragile, yet together they created something beautiful.

Back at the diner, David and Lewis were finishing up their meal. The conversation had shifted to lighter topics, movies they wanted to see, the music they were into, basketball, and plans for the next semester.

"Well, I guess we should head out," David said, glancing at the clock on the wall. It was getting late, and the snow outside showed no signs of stopping.

"Yeah, good call," Lewis agreed, grabbing his coat. "Thanks for tonight, man. I needed this."

"Same here," Lewis said, genuinely meaning it. "If we can, let's do it again before we head back to campus."

"For sure," he replied with a grin. They paid the bill and stepped out into the cold, the snow crunching under their boots as they walked to their cars.

As David got into the cab, he glanced at his phone again, tempted to text Sara. But he hesitated, not sure what he would say. Instead, he pulled out his earphones, told the driver where to drop him off, and played a song. The silence of the snowy night settled around him like a soft embrace.

Sara stood by the window in her room, looking out at the snow-covered yard. The house was quiet now, everyone else having gone to bed. She reached for her phone, scrolling through her messages, stopping when she saw David's name.

Her thumb hovered over the screen, debating whether to text him. But something held her back, a mix of fear and uncertainty. Instead, she put her phone down and climbed into her bed, pulling the covers up to her chin.

As she drifted off to sleep, the image of David lingered in her mind, like the snowflakes falling gently outside, silent, yet impossible to ignore.

The night passed, the snow continuing to fall, covering the world in a quiet, peaceful blanket. David and Sara, miles apart yet connected by unspoken thoughts, lay awake in their respective homes, the future uncertain, but the present wrapped in the calm of the season.

Chapter Ten

The campus was eerily quiet, the kind of quietness that felt unnatural, as if the world had suddenly decided to hold its breath. The usual hum of student life, the distant chatter, the rustling of leaves, and the occasional blare of music from a nearby dorm were conspicuously absent. Most students had either gone home or were holed up in their rooms, exhausted from weeks of studying. But for Ashley, the quiet wasn't a reprieve. It was oppressive, a blanket of stillness that only amplified the noise in her head.

As she sat on the edge of her bed, her gaze fixed on the wall opposite her, she could feel the quiet seeping into her bones, pressing down on her chest until it was hard to breathe. During the day, she could almost convince herself that everything was normal. She would busy herself with menial tasks—organizing her desk, folding laundry—anything to keep her hands moving and her mind occupied.

But now, in the dead of night, with the campus still and dark, there was nothing to distract her. The shadows in her room seemed to stretch and twist, taking on shapes that reminded her of that night. The night she wished she could forget.

Her thoughts started as a trickle, small, insistent whispers at the back of her mind. *I shouldn't have gone to that party.* The thought replayed over and over, a relentless echo that she couldn't muffle. She had known it was a bad idea. Sara had even suggested they stay in, have a quiet night in the dorms with some movies and snacks.

But Ashley had ignored her instincts, pushed aside the small voice that told her to stay where it was safe. Why? Maybe it was the fear of missing out, or perhaps she had just wanted to feel normal for a little while, to forget about the stress of exams and the pressures of school. Whatever the reason, she had gone, and now she was paying the price.

She could still hear the music from that night, loud and pulsating, filling the house with a beat that vibrated through her chest. She had felt dizzy, overwhelmed by the noise, the heat, the press of bodies around her. But she had forced a smile, tried to act like she was having fun. Actually, she was.

Everyone else seemed to be. She remembered seeing Jenna across the room, laughing and dancing, surrounded by people. They had come to the party together, but at some point, Ashley had lost sight of her. She couldn't remember when, exactly. It was all a blur now.

And that's when the questions started. Yeah, the same question anyone who goes out with a friend and ends up being the only one hurt would ask, those funny questions.

'*What happened, Jenna?*' Ashley's mind latched onto the thought, her heart quickening as suspicion began to creep in. '*Where did she go? Why did she leave me alone?*' She searched her memories, trying to piece together the events of the night, but things were getting foggy, distorted by the fear and the alcohol she had consumed to calm her nerves.

Maybe Jenna knew what was going to happen? She could picture her, laughing, smiling, but then—nothing. The thought gnawed at her, growing darker with each passing minute. '*Did she set this up? Was she in on this?*' The idea fit in, but of course, she knew it was absurd. She knew that was a figment of her emotion; she knew right now she was projecting, and it depressed her the most.

Ashley wondered, her mind meandering into paranoia. The campus, once her home, her escape from her mother, now felt like an enemy domain. She had always felt safe here, surrounded by people who were supposed to be her friends, her community. But now, she wasn't.

A lot was going through her mind at once, and she needed something to get these thoughts off her head, but she was out of alcohol or pills; it was just Jenna's remaining bottles of cold medicine on her desk, and she didn't mind risking it.

* * *

The holidays had come and gone, leaving behind a bitter aftertaste that lingered with Sara was en route back to campus. The festive lights, the laughter of family gatherings, and the warmth of holiday meals had done little to lift her spirits.

But she couldn't forget: she had been out with her parents one evening, strolling through the city mall, when she saw him —David. But it wasn't just David. His arm was wrapped around another girl's shoulder, and they were laughing, completely absorbed in each other. The sight hit Sara like a punch to the gut.

She froze, her heart plummeting. The world seemed to wobble for a moment, the festive lights around her dimming as her vision blurred. Without thinking, she turned sharply on her heel and walked away as fast as she could.

Her parents, chatting happily beside her, noticed the sudden change and asked if something was wrong. Sara forced a smile, barely masking her distress, "Umm, nothing serious, I just need to find the ladies' restroom," she mumbled.

They looked at her quizzically but didn't press the issue. As soon as she was out of their sight, she found a quiet corner and let the tears she'd been holding back slip down her cheeks.

The image of David with that girl was seared into her mind. It played on a loop, tormenting her for the rest of the break. Every time she closed her eyes, she saw them together, happy, oblivious to what was going on, or so she thought.

'*So what if I'm the one avoiding and giving him space? He KISSED me, did that mean nothing to him? He's already out and about with different ladies?*' Sara thought. Her thoughts were making her feel more annoyed than jealous.

By the time she was back on campus, she was a bundle of nerves and unresolved emotions. She didn't know how she was going to face David, or even if she wanted to. But before she could even begin to untangle her own feelings, something more urgent was gnawing at her, Ashley. She never took any of her calls or returned any of her messages.

The last time Sara had seen her, something had been off. Ashley had been distant and withdrawn, and Sara's attempts to reach out had been met with silence. Sara had chalked it up to finals stress at first, but now, she knew it was something else, and she wasn't falling for the 'I'm not feeling well".

As soon as she arrived on campus, Sara barely took the time to unload her things. She said goodbye to her parents hastily, giving them quick hugs and reassurances that she would be fine. But as soon as they were out of sight, she sprinted across campus, her heart pounding in her chest, straight to Ashley's dorm.

She couldn't shake the feeling that something was wrong. The thought gnawed at her, driving her forward. When she reached Ashley's dorm, she didn't hesitate. She knocked on the door, at first lightly, and turned the knob to enter, but this time they had actually locked the door. Sara began knocking harder when there was no response.

"Ashley?" she called out, trying to keep the panic from creeping into her voice. But there was no answer.

Her knocks turned into frantic bangs as she called Ashley's name again, louder this time, her voice betraying the fear that was clawing at her. She pressed her ear against the door, straining to hear anything from inside, but there was only silence. Desperation rising,

Sara tried the doorknob again, as if her desperation was the key to access.

"Ashley! Please, open the door!" Sara shouted, her heart racing. She pounded on the door, fear gripping her as the silence continued. She was about to turn and run for help when she heard it—a soft thud from inside the dorm.

Sara froze, her breath catching in her throat. It was faint, but unmistakable. Something, or someone, had moved inside the dorm apartment. "Ashley?" she called again, her voice shaking now. She banged on the door harder, frantic, her mind racing with worst-case scenarios.

It was Ashley's roommate Jenna. With a frantic look on her face, Jenna opened the door, "Geesh, you okay? You banging like you da police."

"I'm sorry, but it's urgent," says Sara, and she brushes past Jenna. She sprinted to Ashley's door, turned the knob, but it was locked. She banged on the door just as fervently as before.

"Please, Ashley, answer me!" she cried, pressing her ear against the door, her heart hammering against her ribs. She could hear her own pulse pounding in her ears, drowning out everything else.

"Ashley, I know you're in there. Why are you avoiding your friends? Your mom? Me?" She paused, feeling emotionally spent, and she sat in front of her room door. "I thought maybe you were having a bad day the last time we talked, and I thought about how rude I was for not asking how your night went. But Ashley, please talk to me. Whatever it is. I am here. God is here." Sadness slowly sat down and joined her. "Nothing is too hard for him to handle, and I am here if you need a listening ear with no judgment. I love you and I mean that. I'm sorry if I did anything to hurt you, but please let me know what's going on. Let me in, please."

The seconds stretched into what felt like hours as Sara stood there, waiting, hoping for any sign from her friend. When there was nothing but silence, a cold dread settled in her stomach. She stood up and backed away from the door, her hands trembling as she pulled out her phone to call for help. But just as she was about to dial, she got a text.

"I'm sleepy, Sara, please go," Sara read.

Her hands shook as she tried the doorknob again, as if somehow, it would magically unlock. But it didn't budge. "Ashley, please, just let me in!" Sara's voice cracked as she pounded on the door one last time, her fists aching from the effort.

Sara slid down the door and sat outside Ashley's room in hopes that Ashley would come out. But after ten minutes, even though Sara didn't want to, she got the point that Ashley wanted to be alone. Sara gathered her strength, stood up, and walked to the main entryway. She thanked Jenna for letting her in and solemnly walked out, closing the door behind her.

While Jenna wasn't sure what was going on, she could sense the heaviness. So, she made her way to Ashley's door, knocked lightly, and spoke softly.

"Hey, I don't know what's going on between you two, but I wanted to make sure you were good, cause Sara walked out of here looking like her dog had died."

Knowing that Sara had left, Ashley opened the door, wrapped herself in a blanket as if she was in the Arctic, and light was her arch nemesis. Jenna could smell a stench coming from Ashley's room. The room was dark, the curtains drawn tightly shut, and the air was thick with an uneasy tension. The room felt more like a cave than the cozy, lived-in space it usually was.

As the door opened, her eyes fell on Ashley, slumped back into her bed, half-buried under a pile of blankets. Her hair was disheveled, her face pale and drawn, and dark circles marred the skin beneath her eyes. She looked like a shadow of the person she used to be, and it set off alarm bells in her roommate's mind.

"Whoa! You look like crap," Jenna blurted out before she could stop herself. "What happened? You sick or something?"

Ashley didn't respond at first. She just stared blankly at the wall, as if she hadn't even heard her. Her roommate frowned, moving closer. "Ashley?" she pressed, her voice softer now, more careful. "Hey, do you need to see someone? They got free counseling services on campus, you know. Cause whatever this is, it's eating away at you."

The words barely seemed to register with Ashley. For a long moment, it was as if she were too far gone to hear or care. Then, suddenly, she snapped, her eyes flashing with a sharp, unexpected anger. "Forget you!" she spat, her voice harsh and raw.

The outburst took her roommate by surprise. She's never seen Ashley like this, so defensive, so on edge. She quickly regained her composure, though, not wanting to escalate things further.

"Look, imma excuse that," she said, her tone firm but not unkind. "But you betta get yourself together. I ain't yo momma, but I will sure whoop your behind if you come at me like that again."

Ashley's anger deflated as quickly as it had risen. She didn't have the energy to fight, not anymore. Her roommate's words barely penetrated the thick fog of exhaustion that hung over her. She just felt tired. So tired that she didn't care about the consequences of her outburst or about anything, really. Everything seemed pointless, like she was going through the motions, a hollow shell of the person she used to be.

Seeing Ashley so defeated, her roommate's irritation quickly gave way to concern again. She wanted to help, but she wasn't sure how. Ashley had always been strong, always the one to brush things off and keep moving forward. Seeing her like this—so broken—was unnerving. But no matter how much she wanted to help, Ashley clearly wasn't in a place where she was willing to accept it.

Jenna decided it was best to give her some space for now. "Alright," she said, her voice softening. "But just know, I'm here if you need me, okay? Don't shut me out, too."

Ashley didn't respond, her eyes already glazing over as she turned back to the wall, retreating into the dark recesses of her mind. Her roommate stood there for a moment longer, unsure of what else to say. Finally, she let out a small sigh and left the room, closing the door behind her as quietly as she could.

* * *

The break had passed in a blur, a brief respite that came and went too quickly. Most students returned to campus with renewed energy, ready to tackle the new semester. But Sara was struck by how different things felt. She had made her way back to her own room after her earlier, frantic attempt to check on Ashley, which left her feeling more helpless than ever. Ashley had refused to see her, shutting her out completely. It was like there was a wall between them, one that Sara couldn't break through, no matter how hard she tried.

Back in her room, Sara sat on her bed, staring at the floor as she replayed the events of the past few days in her mind. She had been so sure that something terrible had happened to Ashley, but getting her text message let her know that Ashley was safe, at least physically. But she was still far from fine. Sara's heart ached for her friend, but she didn't know what else she could do.

Feeling utterly defeated, Sara realized that the only thing left for her to do was pray. She wasn't sure what else could help, but she had always believed in the power of prayer, especially when all other options seemed to fail. She got up from her bed and knelt on the floor, her hands clasped tightly together as she bowed her head.

"Dear God," she began, her voice trembling slightly, "please, watch over Ashley. I don't know what's going on with her, but I know she's hurting. She's in so much pain, and I don't know how to help her. Please, give her the strength to get through this. Help her find peace, and help me to be there for her in whatever way she needs."

Sara's voice wavered as she continued to pray, tears slipping down her cheeks. She prayed for guidance, for wisdom, for anything that would help her reach Ashley. She prayed for David, too, asking for the strength to face him. And most of all, she prayed for herself, for the strength to keep going, to not give up on the people she cared about, no matter how hard things got.

When she finally finished, she stayed there for a moment longer, letting the silence wash over her. There was a certain peace that came with praying, a sense of letting go, even if just for a little while. As she stood up, she felt a little lighter, like a small part of the burden she had been carrying had been lifted.

Sara wiped away her tears and took a deep breath. She knew that the road ahead would be difficult, both for her and for Ashley. But she also knew that she wouldn't give up on her friend. No matter what it took, she would be there for Ashley, even if it meant waiting until she was ready to let her in again.

With softball season in full swing, Sara knew she wouldn't have much time between studying, practices, and games, but she decided to keep reaching out to Ashley, gently, persistently, and with all the patience she could muster. She wouldn't force anything, but she wouldn't disappear either. She hoped that one day, Ashley would see that she wasn't alone, and that there were people who cared about her, people who wouldn't let her go through this on her own.

For now, though, Sara could only wait, and pray, and hope that the friend she loves so dearly would find her way back from the darkness that had consumed her.

Chapter Eleven

The next few weeks were a blur of anxiety and discomfort for Sara. Nothing seemed to make sense anymore. The holidays were supposed to be a time of joy and renewal, but they left her feeling aimless. On top of practices and learning teammates, Sara had enough on her plate.

Her friendship with Ashley, something she had always relied on, felt like it was slipping away. They had never had a fallout like this before. Sure, there had been disagreements. Everyone has those, but nothing so serious that it would keep them from speaking for weeks.

She wondered what could have gone wrong. Did it happen before or after the party? Whatever it was had to be serious. Ashley had never been like this, even when she had altercations with her mom. It was more than that, and she needed help.

So many things went through her mind at once. Sara found herself replaying their last interaction over and over in her mind. She could still see the anger in Ashley's eyes, the way she had lashed out at her, the bitterness in her voice when she had told Sara to let her be.

It was like a saber in Sara's heart, twisting deeper every time she thought about it. She kept wondering what she had done wrong, why

Ashley was shutting her out so thoroughly. The uncertainty gnawed at her, making it hard to concentrate on anything else.

And then there was her not knowing how to face David; at least she was having a taste of her own medicine —she knew how it felt to be avoided. The difference was that David wasn't making any effort; in fact, he found peace in the arms of so many other ladies. That's what she gets for falling for a ladies' man.

In an attempt to manage her emotions, Sara began avoiding certain areas of the campus, especially those where she knew David might be. Which wasn't hard because softball practices required her to take a different route, but practice wasn't every day. She couldn't bear the thought of running into him, not after what she had seen over the holidays. The memory of him with that other girl was still fresh in her mind, a constant source of pain. She didn't need any more stress in her life, and seeing David would only make things worse.

But even with her best efforts, Sara struggled to focus in class and even on the field. Every time she entered a lecture hall or sat down to study, her mind wandered to Ashley. She would glance over at the empty seat where Ashley usually sat, feeling a pang of worry. Ashley hadn't been to class in weeks. Ashley did many things, but she never missed classes, even if she attended a party the night before. Ashley wasn't okay; she was going through something. Sara's thoughts spiraled, filled with self-doubt and concern.

"Maybe I did something wrong? What then?" Sara whispered to herself one afternoon, staring blankly at her notebook. Her notes were a mess, words scribbled aimlessly across the page as she tried to make sense of the lecture. But her mind wasn't on the class; it was on Ashley, on their fractured friendship, and on the guilt that was beginning to weigh her down.

She sighed, closing her notebook with a frustrated snap. She was in the campus library, and the quiet surroundings offered little solace. Students around her were focused, heads bent over textbooks and laptops, completely absorbed in their work. But no matter how hard

Sara tried, she couldn't bring herself to care about her studies. Not when Ashley was like that.

As the days passed, Sara found herself turning to prayer more and more. It was the only thing that offered her any comfort. At first, her prayers had been focused on herself, pleas for guidance, for understanding, for a way to fix what was wrong between her and Ashley. But as time went on, she realized that her prayers needed to shift focus.

"God," she whispered one evening, kneeling beside her bed, her hands clasped tightly together. The room was dark, the only light coming from the small lamp on her desk. "I've been praying so much about my own feelings, but I know now that this isn't about me. It's about Ashley. Whatever she's going through, I pray that she gets the help she needs, even if it doesn't come from me."

Sara's voice trembled as she continued, her words heartfelt. "You know all things and see all things, God. If there is anything I need to do to make this situation better, please reveal it to me. Help me to be a better reflection of You, to offer love and support in the way that Ashley needs it."

As she prayed, Sara felt a sense of peace come over her. It wasn't a complete relief; her worries about Ashley hadn't vanished, but it was something. It was a reminder that she wasn't alone, that there was a higher power at work, even if she couldn't see it. She rose from her knees and climbed into bed, her heart a little lighter.

While Sara struggled with feelings of helplessness and guilt, Ashley sank deeper into a pit of despair. The weeks following the holidays had been some of the darkest of her life. She felt as though she were trapped in a nightmare, one she couldn't wake up from, no matter how hard she tried.

Every morning, the same routine played out. Ashley would open her eyes, staring blankly at the ceiling for what felt like hours before finally rolling over in bed. The room was always dark. She couldn't stand the sunlight anymore. It felt too harsh, too bright for the place she was in. The thought of getting up, of facing the world, was too much to bear. All she could manage was to curl back up under the blankets, retreating into the small, dark world she had created for herself.

Her appetite had disappeared almost entirely. She couldn't remember the last time she had eaten a decent meal. The thought of food made her stomach churn. The most she could do was nibble on a piece of toast or a granola bar, just enough to keep the gnawing hunger at bay. But even that was a struggle. More often than not, she just lay in bed, too exhausted to move, too tired to care.

And then there were the thoughts, the relentless punishing thoughts that plagued her day and night. They were like a constant, inescapable storm in her mind, swirling with guilt, shame, and self-loathing. She replayed the events of that party over and over, the memories haunting her, refusing to let her go.

Why had she gone? Why hadn't she stayed in the dorm with Sara, safe and sound? Why had she let herself get caught up in the excitement, in the thrill of something new? Why hadn't she been able to stop it? Why hadn't she screamed louder, fought harder? The questions tormented her, each one a blade twisting in her heart.

"I'm no good," she muttered to herself one night, lying in bed, staring at the ceiling. The room was silent, save for the faint hum of the heater.

Her voice was flat, devoid of any emotion. It was as though she were stating a simple fact, something she had come to accept. She closed her eyes, trying to block out the thoughts, but they only grew louder, more insistent.

She hadn't left her dorm room for quite some time. The days blended, a monotonous cycle of sleeping, waking, and numbing herself with cough syrup. The medicine was the only thing that brought her any semblance of relief. It wasn't alcohol, but it was enough to make her drowsy, to dull the edges of the pain just enough to let her sleep.

But even that was losing its effectiveness. The syrup didn't bring the same comfort it once had. It was as though her body had built up a tolerance to it, the darkness in her mind too bottomless for the medicine to reach. She was tired of everything, tired of the pain, the thoughts, the loneliness. But most of all, she was tired of herself.

One day, as she lay in bed, staring at the bottle of the almost-empty cough syrup on her nightstand, the words of her roommate came back to her. They had been echoing in the back of her mind for days, but she had tried to ignore them. But they became impossible to push away.

"Do you need to see someone? They got free counseling services on campus, you know?"

The words had been spoken with concern, but Ashley had been too wrapped up in her own misery to appreciate it. Now they resonated with her. Maybe her roommate was right. Perhaps she did need help, help she couldn't give herself.

Ashley sat up in bed, the movement slow and deliberate. Her body felt heavy, as though weighed down by an invisible force. She glanced around the room, taking in the mess she had let accumulate. Dirty clothes were piled up in the corner, and empty food wrappers littered the floor. The sight made her feel even more hopeless.

She swung her legs over the side of the bed, and her feet touched the cold floor. It took all her strength to stand, to force herself to move. But she did it. She attempted to look presentable and, step by step, made her way to the door, her body protesting with every movement. Her hand trembled as she reached for the doorknob, her mind filled with doubts.

What if they couldn't help me? What if I was too far gone? The questions clawed at her, trying to pull her back into bed, into the darkness. But she ignored them, pushing the door open and stepping out into the common area of their dorm.

The light was harsh, blinding after weeks spent in darkness. Ashley winced, her eyes watered as she adjusted to the brightness. She hadn't been out of her room in so long that it felt foreign, like stepping into a different world. But she kept moving, one foot in front of the other, making her way to the counseling office.

It was late in the afternoon, and the campus was quiet. Most students were in class or studying, leaving the hallways eerily empty. Ashley's footsteps echoed off the walls as she walked, her heart pounding in her chest. She felt like she was on the brink of collapse, but she kept going, driven by something she couldn't quite name. When she finally reached the counseling office, she saw a door with the doctor's name on it. She hesitated. The door was right in front of her.

"Hey," she heard someone call from behind her as she turned. "You have to book a session before you can go in. You can come with me to the counter. The young lady continued to walk to her desk without fully looking at Ashley. She handed her a clipboard with some paperwork to fill out. Ashley's mumble and grunt broke the young lady's focus long enough for her to look up and see how off-putting Ashley looked.

Sensing something was off, "If you want, I can book one for you as Dr. Evans is free at the moment." The young lady added. Ashley didn't have the strength to utter a word, so she nodded and just followed the lady quietly.

The sound of her knock sent shivers down her spine. "Come in," she heard Dr. Evans say as she held the doorknob. She opened the door, and with each step toward the seat, Ashley wondered what she was doing there.

Chapter Twelve

Lewis jogged along the familiar paths of his university campus, his breath steady and his mind clear. He needed to stop thinking about Sara. While it's only been a couple of weeks since he's seen her, it's been months since high school, and she has chosen to be with David. He didn't understand why she chose David over him no one did.

He was just a friend to her, and he had to accept it despite how hurt he felt. It was late, probably too late for a jog, but it was the only time he had to himself these days. The night air was crisp and cool, a welcome respite from the day's heat. He enjoyed the solitude, the way the campus transformed into a quiet, almost serene place once the sun went down.

All of a sudden, flashes of red and blue lights and the siren of a police car broke the tranquility. Lewis slowed his pace, puzzled. The campus police were a common sight, but he couldn't think of anything that would make the police stop him. He pulled out his earbuds, the music abruptly cutting off as the car approached.

"Hey, what's going on?" Lewis called out, trying to sound casual. Two officers, one tall and burly with a stern expression, the other shorter and stockier, got out of the car and approached him. "Is there a problem, officers?" Lewis asked, trying to keep his voice steady.

"We got a report of a robbery, and you fit the description," the tall officer said, his hand resting on his holstered gun as he looked disgustingly at Lewis.

Lewis was confused. "Robbery? I'm just jogging around campus. I have my student ID right here," he said, as he reached into his pocket to pull out his ID card.

"Keep your hands where I can see them, Nigga!" the shorter officer barked, stepping closer like he was about to blow his head off.

Lewis's heart sank; he knew what this was about. These men were racist, and he was labeled suspicious for the mere fact that his skin had more melanin than theirs. A rage of anger mixed with fear welled inside of him. "Excuse me, I'm just trying to show you my ID. I'm a student here."

The tall officer grabbed Lewis's arm and roughly pulled it behind his back. "You think you're smart, huh? We've seen your kind play the innocent student card. Let's see some ID."

Lewis got upset, but remained calm. He felt bullied and helpless. They didn't hide that they were attacking him because of his looks. *"Your kind"? You've got to be kidding*, he thought. Wincing in pain, he managed to pull his ID out of his pocket. The officer snatched it from his hand and examined it under the flashlight.

All right, Lewis Henderson. What are you doing out here this late?" the tall officer demanded.

"I already told you. I'm just jogging. Am I not allowed to jog? I live in the dorms right over there!" Lewis said, nodding towards the building. His hands shivered from the pain and anger he felt.

"Yeahhhh, you want to hit me? You trying to be rough with me? You think I'm scared of you?" The tall officer taunted Lewis as he pulled on Lewis's arm.

"Scared of me?" Lewis asked, forcing the words out of his mouth. Fear had crept in, and he was suppressing the urge to fight back. He's heard and seen on the news how things like this could pan out. Black man painted as the villain, when truly he was the victim.

"We've had reports of break-ins and vandalism around here. You fit the description."

"No! This is ridiculous! I'm not breaking into anything. I'm a student. Look, my ID has my dorm address on it." Lewis defended.

The tall officer shoved the ID back into Lewis's hand. "Doesn't matter. You're coming with us. Explain yourself at the station."

Lewis was still trying to comprehend what exactly was going on, as the shorter officer forcefully pushed Lewis against the hood of the car and handcuffed him.

"You have the right to remain silent," he began, reciting the Miranda rights mechanically.

"You do not have any right to do this!" Lewis struggled.

"I will blow your brains out"! The tall officer shouted sternly. Lewis didn't want to be a victim of their brutality; he didn't want anything more than this. He followed them quietly. "You people always think you can get away with anything."

Lewis's eyes widened, not being able to dismiss what the officer said this time. "What do you mean by 'you people'?"

"You know exactly what I mean," the officer replied coldly, and as the other continued reciting the Miranda rights.

There was the confirmation he needed that this wasn't about any report; they weren't doing their "jobs". They clearly were being racist, and it disgusted him.

On a Thursday night, Lewis found himself in a cold, uncomfortable, gray holding cell at the local police station. His wrists were sore from the handcuffs, and his mind was racing. He couldn't believe that this was happening. He had heard of racial profiling on the news, but never did he think that it would show up on his front door. Never did he imagine that it would be him. He had done nothing wrong, and yet here he was.

His emotions were like a dam with cracks too fine to see. With each step in the booking process—mugshot, fingerprints, paperwork—

water begins to seep through those cracks. He felt himself losing it, his soul crumbling away. He replayed a conversation he had with some students within the first month of being on campus.

Kourtney and James were part of the African American Student Collation for Justice Union, and when all campus organizations were out in the courtyard recruiting for new members of various causes, he waved them off. Lewis made a lasting impression on him because he told them all that what they were doing wasn't necessary and their activities would cause unnecessary issues. Later that week, he realized he had a class with Kourtney and James. Oddly enough, they had another conversation, and they actually bonded.

And while he didn't join their organization, he built a bond with them and understood where they were coming from. But now, he had experienced firsthand what they were trying to warn him about.

In high school, racism wasn't a thing. There was classism based on the amount of money that your family had, but Lewis never really got into that thing. He never had to because his parents were financially well off. While Lewis was humble about it all, his family's wealth spoke for him. But in a place where he wasn't known, his money didn't matter, and his color spoke before he did.

The next morning, word of Lewis's arrest spread quickly across campus. It happened that one of the members of ASCJU interned at the police station. Students were shocked and outraged, especially Kourtney and James. The ASCJU convened an emergency meeting to discuss their response.

"We can't let this go unchallenged," Kourtney, the ASCJU president, said, her voice filled with determination. "We all know Lewis was arrested for no reason other than the color of his skin, and we can't be silent about this. We need to take action."

"Exactly," James agreed. "We need to protest and demand his release. Racial profiling and police brutality injustice can't continue."

The room buzzed with agreement, and plans for a protest began to take shape. Posters were made, social media campaigns were launched, and students from all backgrounds came together to show their support.

Monday morning, the campus was transformed into a sea of posters and flags. Hundreds of students gathered in front of the administration building, chanting slogans like "No justice, no peace!", "Say no to police brutality", "My only crime is that I'm black", and "Free Lewis now!"

Kourtney took the stage, her voice amplified by a megaphone. "We are here today to stand against racism and police brutality. Our friend and fellow student, Lewis, was unjustly arrested, and we demand his immediate release!"

The crowd roared in approval, their voices echoing across the campus. James stepped forward. "I've known Lewis for quite a while. He's one of the hardest-working and honest people I know. What happened to him is a clear example of racial profiling. We won't stop until he's free and justice is served!"

The protest continued throughout the day, with students sharing their own experiences of discrimination and calling for change.

Chapter Thirteen

Unfocused and tired from practice, Sara didn't realize she had unconsciously taken the route she swore to avoid. Her thoughts were tangled in a web of worry and confusion, replaying the last conversation she'd had with Ashley, every subtle sign she might have missed. It wasn't until she sat down on a bench, trying to gather her thoughts, that she noticed David approaching from a distance. Sara's heart raced as she caught sight of David, panic gripped her, and she quickly scanned the area, hoping for a quick exit. She didn't want to face him, not now, not with everything she had swirling in her mind.

She glanced to her right, noticing a small path that led through the campus gardens. Maybe she could slip away unnoticed. But as she took a step in that direction, a group of students wandered down the path, their chatter filling the air. It would be too obvious if she bolted now.

Her eyes darted to the left, where the entrance to a nearby building stood. She could duck inside, pretend she had somewhere to be, but the doors were too far. By the time she'd reached them, David would have already seen her.

There was no escape. The realization hit her like a wave, and she felt a tightening in her chest. She was trapped. Sara's mind raced, desperately searching for a way to avoid this confrontation, but every option felt impossible. David was getting closer, and she could almost feel the weight of his gaze. There was no avoiding it now. She was out of time.

With a deep breath, she resigned herself to the inevitable and sank deeper into the bench, hoping that maybe, just maybe, David would pay no attention to her, but she heard his voice, and her heart sank further.

"Hey, you okay?"

As much as she wanted to avoid him, hearing his voice was healing to her bleeding heart. She looked up, squinting against the sun as it shone in her face. She raised a hand to shield her eyes and saw David standing there, concern etched on his face.

"Hey, you okay?" David repeated. His voice was gentle, filled with concern, and it cut through her like a knife.

"No," she admitted, her voice heavy with the weight of everything she'd been carrying, including her softball gear. "Have you spoken to Ashley lately?"

"Naw. Now that I think about it, I haven't talked to her since we left for break. What's up?"

"I'm worried about her," Sara began, her voice trembling slightly. "The day after the party, she lashed out at me for no reason. Then she lied to her mom about riding home with me during winter break and stayed here on campus. I only found that out when I went to her house to look for her. When I got back on campus, I went to her dorm room, and she avoided talking to me even when I knew she was in there."

"Yeah, that don't sound like her," David replied, shaking his head. "Y'all like best friends. Y'all didn't get into it, did y'all?"

"No. I mean, she's missed weeks of class now."

"Ashley, missing class? That's definitely not her. Imma give her a call—but other than that, how have you been?"

Sara, hearing the tone of his voice change, hesitated, not wanting to shift the focus onto herself but knowing she couldn't avoid it forever. "I mean, I'm alright."

David raised an eyebrow, not buying it. "You sure? 'Cause you're pretty much avoiding me the same way Ashley is avoiding you."

Her heart skipped a beat. "Hold on. What do you mean?"

"I saw you downtown, back at home," David said, his voice calm but firm. "You busted that U-turn, trying to avoid me. Then you didn't come to the diner like we all agreed. You texted Lewis instead of me, like my phone don't work. I mean, come on, I ain't slow. You been like this since our last study session. Did I do something wrong?"

Feeling a wave of discomfort, Sara looked down, away from David, fiddling with her hands. The truth had been simmering inside her, but saying it out loud felt like exposing herself in a way she wasn't ready for. But David's patience, his willingness to listen, pushed her to confront what she'd been avoiding.

"Come on, Sara," David urged gently. "Tell me what's going on in that mind of yours. Don't shut me out."

"Okay!" she finally blurted out, signaling to him to give her a moment to gather her thoughts. She took a deep breath, steeling herself. "Our last study session was great— yet scary."

"Scary?" David echoed, clearly puzzled.

Sara locked eyes with him, signaling that this was serious and that he needed to listen. "I've never been with anyone—in that way. And I don't want to, anytime soon. I see you with plenty of girls, and I see how they look at you, what they do for you. I'm not like that. I want my first time to be special and with my husband. Ever since I saw you, I liked you, but I can tell you aren't the type of guy to wait. So I didn't want to lead you on that night or for things to get out of hand, so I needed you to go. I didn't know what else to do. Plus, you didn't show up the next day for our study session." She looked at him, her eyes searching his face for any sign of understanding.

"You finished now?" David asked softly, waiting for her nod.

"One. My bad. The next day, I got caught up with Coach and the guys, and it slipped my mind. Two. I'm kinda disappointed that you think I'm the type that can't wait. I'm out here being me, but I was waiting on you. I get it, and I'm feeling you. And I think you're worth the wait."

Sara's heart skipped again, this time from the warmth in his voice. "I'm worth the wait?"

"Yeah."

"So?"

"So?"

"So, what does this mean?" she leaned in.

"What is it that you want?"

Sara hesitated, the vulnerability of the moment sinking in. But this was David—someone who had always been honest with her. She owed him the same. "I want you. I want to be with you. Hold up, not in that way. But I want us to be a couple."

David stood up, positioning himself directly in front of her. He looked into her eyes, his gaze steady, and took her hand in his. "Sara, will you be my old lady?"

"Old lady?" Sara repeated the unfamiliar term.

David smirked, realizing his slang hadn't landed. "Sara, will you be my girl?"

Sara felt a blush creep up her cheeks, a smile breaking through her uncertainty. "Yes, I'll be your old lady."

They both laughed, the tension easing as he sat back down. The air around them seemed lighter, as if the weight of unspoken words had been lifted. They sat in comfortable silence for a while, letting the moment linger.

As they sat together, Sara's thoughts drifted back to Ashley. The worry still gnawed at her, but now there was something else—a sense of hope. She had David by her side, and maybe, just maybe, together they could figure out how to help Ashley.

David seemed to sense her shifting thoughts. "We'll figure out what's going on with Ashley," he said, squeezing her hand gently. "Whatever it is, we'll get through it together."

Sara nodded, feeling a small but significant sense of relief. "Thank you, David. For everything."

"Always," he replied, his voice steady and reassuring.

They continued to sit there, talking about everything and nothing, letting the afternoon sun bathe them in its warmth. The world around them seemed to fade away, leaving just the two of them in a moment that felt like the beginning of something new and hopeful.

Chapter Fourteen

Ashley sat in Dr. Evans' office, her hands tightly clasped in her lap. This wasn't going as easily as she had thought it would. Her life had been a wreck, but she never thought it would land her in a counselor's office.

Dr. Evans had kind, intelligent eyes and a warm demeanor. Her short, curly brown hair framed her face, and she wore a simple yet elegant outfit that radiated professionalism and approachability.

She took a deep breath, trying to find the words to break the ice. It's been five minutes since Ashley walked in and said hello to her. Ashley had only told Dr. Evans her name, and that was all. She noticed the instant regret that enveloped Ashley, the kind you feel when you go to the supermarket and end up buying the things you didn't budget for.

The "what the heck am I doing here?" was so loud, even as Ashley questioned if she had spoken out loud.

"Ashley, I can see that something is weighing heavily on you," Dr. Evans said gently. "Can you tell me what's been going on?"

Ashley hesitated, feeling the familiar wave of shame wash over her. "I just—I feel so down about everything. School, life, it all feels overwhelming."

"It's okay to feel that way. Sometimes, talking about the specifics can help. Is there a particular issue you've been avoiding?"

Ashley bit her lip, her voice barely a whisper. "I'm embarrassed about it."

"You don't need to feel embarrassed here," Dr. Evans reassured her. "This is a safe space."

Ashley sighed, "Maybe next time," she said, forcing a small smile.

Dr. Evans had been the school counselor for more than ten years now, and the look Ashley had was the same look she'd seen before, in the eyes of a former patient. She remembered that the young lady had walked into her office, her eyes cast downward, avoiding any direct gaze. The corners of her eyes were tinged with a subtle redness, betraying the many sleepless nights and silent tears.

Her lashes, heavy with unshed tears, quivered slightly as she blinked, trying to hold them back. When she did glance up, her eyes held a look of hatred, profound shame, a dullness, revealing a depth of loneliness that seemed to swallow the light.

The shadows under her eyes deepened, and her brow furrowed slightly, as if the weight of her thoughts were too heavy to bear. The sadness in her eyes was unmistakable—a silent cry for connection and understanding, yet also a fear of judgment and rejection.

Dr. Evans, not wanting to push it, nodded, her gaze compassionate. "Whenever you're ready," Dr. Evans said warmly. "We'll work through it together. So tell me about your classes, your friends, your dreams, or whatever you want to talk about."

Ashley opened up about her friends David and Sara's complicated relationship, which she didn't understand, and other nuances to fill the time. The session ended, and Ashley stood up, feeling a mixture of relief and frustration. Relief that she was able to talk to someone, but frustrated that the conversation had nothing to do with her issue. She spent pretty much all her session talking about her friends. "Thank you for your time, Dr. Evans."

"Of course, Ashley. I look forward to our next session," Dr. Evans replied. "Take care."

Ashley walked into the reception area, the weight of the session lifting slightly. She approached the receptionist's window to make her next appointment. Ashley watched as the receptionist entered the appointment into the system. She thanked her and left the office. As she was leaving the building, she accidentally bumped into another woman, causing the woman to drop her clipboard.

"Oh, I'm so sorry!" Ashley exclaimed, bending down to pick it up. The other woman did the same, and their hands brushed as they reached for the clipboard.

Their eyes met, and Ashley felt something unexpected, a sudden jolt. The woman exuded quiet confidence that drew her in, and her perfume smelled wonderful. They stared at each other for an uncomfortable amount of time, a connection sparking between them.

"Sorry again," Ashley said, finally breaking the silence with a small smile.

"It's okay," the woman assured her, smiling back. "Accidents happen, and no one got hurt. So, everyone's okay."

Ashley smirked, feeling a strange warmth from the woman's words. "Yeah, we are." She stood up and handed the clipboard back to the woman.

"Thanks," the woman said, still smiling.

Ashley nodded, turning to walk out the door. As she exited, she couldn't resist glancing back. There was something about the woman that made her heart race—a feeling that she couldn't quite explain.

"What is wrong with you?" she muttered to herself as she left.

* * *

Rebecca stepped in, a smile playing on her lips. It had been years since her last session with Dr. Evans, and she felt a world apart from the troubled student she once was. Her eyes, now clear and bright, looked through the familiar room, landing on Dr. Evans, who looked up from her desk with a welcoming smile.

"Rebecca! It's so good to see you," Dr. Evans said. She was surprised to see Rebecca here; she had only just thought of her.

"It's good to see you, too, Dr. Evans. I hope you don't mind me popping in." Rebecca replied, shaking her hand warmly. She sat down in the chair she had occupied countless times before, feeling a comfortable sense of nostalgia.

"Not at all. You look well," Dr. Evans observed, her eyes twinkling with genuine pleasure. "How have you been?"

She took a deep breath, her smile widening. "I've been good. Really good, actually. Life has changed so much in these years. I feel content— at peace. There were times I never thought I'd feel this way again—happy.

Dr. Evans smiled warmly. "You've come a long way. I'm so proud of you."

"Thank you," Rebecca said, her voice soft with emotion. "I couldn't have done it without you. I didn't want to take up much of your time. I wanted you to know that I got a position as an Assistant Professor here."

"Congratulations! Dr. Evans was proud of her. They chatted for a brief moment, and Rebecca left, having to get to an appointment.

That night, Ashley lay in her bed, her thoughts drifting back to the woman she had bumped into. There was something about her that she couldn't shake. She felt a flicker of curiosity, a desire to know more about her. For the first time in weeks, she was able to fall asleep without self-medicating— dreaming about the lady she had bumped into, and in between thoughts, she wondered why.

Chapter Fifteen

Rebecca was leaving the campus after finishing a meeting. It was late evening, the sun casting a warm glow on the bustling university grounds. As she walked, her eyes caught sight of Ashley sitting alone on a bench near the library. Rebecca's heart sank.

The way Ashley was looking, she figured something was disturbing her peace. Determined to help, she approached her with a warm, inviting smile. "Hey," Rebecca called out, waving as she drew closer. She wished she had known her name, but her calling out was enough to grab her attention.

Ashley looked up. Her eyes and smile were wide with surprise. It was the same lady she had bumped into. "Oh, hi," she replied eagerly. In that moment, her heart began to race like a jockey on a horse, but she settled herself. The feelings she was experiencing are all new, and she didn't want to seem awkward or over the top. So she dialed back her smile.

Rebecca sat down beside her, maintaining a comfortable distance. "I hope this doesn't sound strange, but I've been thinking about our brief encounter." Catching herself and trying to rephrase it, she stumbled over her words. "What I meant to say is that seeing you just now reminded me of that same look you had when I saw you in the office. Is everything alright?" she asked, trying to keep her tone light.

The question made Ashley feel vulnerable. She shrugged, staring at her hands clasped in her lap. "I've just been...busy, I guess."

Rebecca nodded, sensing the walls Ashley had built around herself. She knew pushing too hard would only make Ashley retreat further.

"Whatever it is, I hope you know that I care about you," Rebecca said, stopping abruptly. It's like a cloud was hovering over her, hindering her ability to think. "Gosh, I hope I don't sound creepy, but I guess concerned would be a better fit. You have someone who's concerned about you?"

Ashley laughed painfully. All her life, she didn't know what it meant to be cared for, well, except for the guys who "cared" for her as long as they were getting laid. Sara? She was too busy with David and Jesus. Her father was only financially there, making sure she had everything she needed, but he was not there for her time or attention. Ashley's eyes flickered with emotion, but she quickly looked away. She didn't want to seem rude or insensitive, so she shook herself and extended her hand.

"My name is Ashley," Ashley responded, "and I'm fine. Just dealing with some stuff."

Rebecca took a deep breath. "Oh, Ashley! Nice meeting you— again. A pleasure to finally know your name. If you ever want to talk, I'm here for you. No judgment, no pressure. Just someone concerned." Rebecca added.

There was a long pause; the silence between them was filled with unspoken words. Finally, Ashley took a shaky breath and stared into her eyes. She felt a rush of warmth —something she didn't usually feel— well, except when she was with Jay in junior year. She kept staring at Rebecca, as if she had asked a question and was waiting for an answer. She had told Rebecca her name and was expecting an introduction as well.

"Oh. I'm Rebecca! Sorry." Rebecca said sincerely.

"Something happened to me." Ashley let out. She didn't know how the words left her mouth. All she knew was that she had this strange yet familiar connection with this woman.

Rebecca's heart ached for Ashley. Some years ago, she'd been in a situation where she felt stuck in life. She knew how it felt to be lost and lonely. She placed a comforting hand on Ashley's shoulder. "It's okay, Ashley. You can tell me."

Tears welled up in Ashley's eyes as she struggled to find the words. She didn't feel embarrassed. She felt seen, like she could open up, finally. The dam that had been holding back this secret was ready to be broken. "I...I was raped," she admitted, her voice breaking.

Rebecca's grip on Ashley's shoulder tightened, her own eyes filling with tears and rage. "Oh my God, Ashley, I'm so sorry. I can't imagine what you're going through."

Ashley sniffled, brushing her eyes with the back of her hand. "I don't know what to do. I feel so lost."

Rebecca gently rubbed Ashley's back. "You don't have to go through this alone. Have you spoken to anyone else about what happened?"

Ashley shook her head. "No. I'm ashamed. I don't want people to look at me differently."

Rebecca's heart broke more as her situation and feelings were all too familiar to her. "I understand, but you need support. Have you thought about telling Dr. Evans, the campus counselor? She's really good at helping people through tough times. I know because she's helped me."

"Let me guess. You're a senior?" Ashley asked. When she bumped into her and the clipboard fell, she assumed she was staff.

But because of Rebecca's achievements, she was often mistaken for a student. She was very accomplished for her age. She had graduated from high school at fourteen, received her bachelor's at seventeen, and her master's at nineteen. She earned a PhD, published her first peer-reviewed article at twenty-three, and became an assistant professor at this college at twenty-four.

She was very sought out and even called a visionary by some. Yet Rebecca's past made it hard for her to adjust to college. During her first few years at the college, she frequently visited Dr. Evans, as she helped her through a lot. Rebecca discovered that she struggled to understand emotional safety as separate from romantic connection.

Despite all that, Rebecca had a radiant, porcelain complexion that seemed to shimmer in the sunlight. Her eyes were a bewitching shade of blue, reminiscent of a clear summer sky, and they glistened with warmth and espionage. High cheekbones and a gentle smile gave her an air of grace and kindness. She had a slender, elegant build, with a natural poise and confidence that drew Ashley. Not leaving out her effortless charm and sophistication that made her presence both calming and inspiring.

For a moment, Rebecca got scared. She didn't want to scare her off by telling her she was staff. "Yes," she blurted out, but in an instant, a feeling of regret enveloped her. She shouldn't have lied, but Rebecca felt like it was worth the risk. She was drawn to Ashley.

Ashley tensed up. "I don't know if I can do that. It's too hard to talk about."

Rebecca nodded, understanding her hesitation. "I get it, Ashley. But Dr. Evans can really help you. You don't have to do this alone. I'll go with you if you want."

Ashley looked at Rebecca, her eyes filled with a mix of fear and hope. "You'd do that for me?"

Rebecca smiled warmly. "Of course. We're friends," Pausing, waiting to get confirmation. "And friends help each other. Let's take this one step at a time, okay?" Rebecca thought it only right to exchange contact information if they truly were going to be 'friends'.

Ashley felt the walls built up, chipping away. Wanting to put this trauma behind her but afraid to face it head-on, she nodded. "Okay. I'll think about it."

Rebecca hugged her tightly. "Take all the time you need. I'm here for you."

* * *

Later that evening, David and Sara were enjoying a quiet moment together in the campus garden. The setting sun painted the sky in shades of pink and orange, casting a romantic glow over the scene. David pulled Sara closer, his arm wrapped around her shoulders.

"You know, I've always loved this time of day," David said, smiling down at Sara. "Everything looks so," finding the right word to match the moment, "beautiful."

Sara leaned into him, a content smile on her face. "It's perfect. Just like you."

David smirked, "Are you flirting?" he asked, expressing surprise.

"Ummm," Sara shied away.

Pressing a kiss to her temple. "You're the perfect one, Sara."

They sat in comfortable silence for a few moments before Sara's expression grew serious. "David, I'm really worried about Ashley. She's still not returning my calls or texts."

David nodded, his brow furrowing. "Yeah, she hasn't answered or returned my calls either. Have you been by her place?"

Sara sighed. "I've tried, but they started locking their door, and every time I knock, her roommate answers and says she's not there. I don't know what to do."

David took her hand, his thumb gently rubbing over her knuckles. "Just be patient and let her know you're there for her. She'll reach out when she's ready."

Sara leaned her head against his shoulder, taking comfort in his words. "I hope you're right."

* * *

The next day, Rebecca met up with Ashley again, this time in a restaurant off campus. They ordered their drinks and found a corner to sit.

"So, I've been thinking about what you said," Ashley began, her voice hesitant. "About telling Dr. Evans."

Rebecca smiled encouragingly. "That's good, Ashley. It's a big step, but you're not alone. Remember, I'll be with you every step of the way."

Ashley took a deep breath. "Okay. I'll do it. I'll talk to her."

Rebecca reached across the table and squeezed Ashley's hand. "You're so brave, Ashley. I'm proud of you."

Ashley managed a small smile. "Thank you, Rebecca. I truly appreciate your support."

Sara was ordering when she saw Ashley smiling with someone. Sara wondered who she was and what was going on. Sara figured that while this might not be the best time, this would be perhaps the only time she'll have to talk to Ashley.

Not wanting to waste this moment, Sara walked off before getting her order. She was so laser-focused on reaching Ashley that she didn't see the chair that wasn't fully pushed in and bumped right into it. The chair screeched across the floor as Sara stumbled. The noise was enough to draw Ashley's attention away from Rebecca.

Ashley scanned the area from which the noise came and saw Sara walking toward her. Ashley pulled her hand away from Rebecca's. Sara noticed Ashley's withdrawal and nervous expression. Ashley gathered her things quickly and took off before Sara could reach her. Sara called out to Ashley, but that only seemed to make Ashley move faster. *Was this why Ashley was pushing her away? Why is she avoiding me?* Sara thought.

Rebecca, not sure what was happening, was puzzled when Ashley got up and ran off. It wasn't until Sara was in the general area that she realized Ashley was avoiding someone. And since Ashley had departed quickly, she figured she should, too. Rebecca was still finding her footing in this new role, and anyone thinking she was romantically involved with a student would be like her walking on thin ice. One wrong move and things could crack and fall from under her. She needed to be cautious.

* * *

The day for Ashley's next appointment came, and Rebecca had come to support her. They had gone a few yards from the office when she told Ashley that the next few steps were critical for Ashley and that she needed to take them alone. Rebecca assured her that she'll stay right here, but walking into the office was her way of taking control of the situation—of regaining her power. Ashley agreed, and Rebecca offered a reassuring smile, silent support as Ashley walked into the reception area.

Ashley found herself sitting in Dr. Evans's office, Dr. Evans smiling at Ashley. "Hello, Ashley. It's nice to see you again." Dr. Evans said, her voice calm and soothing. "How are you feeling today?"

Ashley swallowed hard, her nerves threatening to overwhelm her. "I'm...nervous," she admitted.

"That's perfectly okay," Dr. Evans replied. "This is a secure space, and you can take your time. Would you like to start by telling me what's been going on?"

Ashley nodded, taking a deep breath. "I-I was raped," she said, her voice barely above a whisper.

Dr. Evans's expression remained gentle and understanding. "Thank you for sharing that with me, Ashley. I'm so sorry that happened to you. It's incredibly brave of you to talk about it."

Tears filled Ashley's eyes; it felt as if a boulder had fallen from her shoulders as she continued.

"I've been feeling so lost and alone. I didn't know who to turn to. My friends are too invested in their relationship with each other. Yet, my mom is a drunk who doesn't miss any opportunity to embarrass me. I've been avoiding people because I feel like they would judge me." She poured out her heart.

Dr. Evans nodded. "It's completely normal to feel that way after such a traumatic experience. But you're not alone. You have help and resources available to you."

Ashley sniffled, wiping her eyes. "I don't want people to look at me differently."

Dr. Evans leaned forward slightly, her gaze empathetic. "It's natural to worry about how others might react, but it's important to remember that what happened to you doesn't define who you are. You're still the same person, and you deserve support and understanding."

Ashley took a shaky breath. "I'm scared. I don't know how to move forward. I'm reminded every day of what happened. If a guy gets close to me, I freeze."

Dr. Evans nodded. "Healing is a process, and it takes time. But you're taking the first step by reaching out for help. We can work together to find ways to cope and heal."

"Have you told any of your friends yet?"

Ashley looked down, her voice barely above a whisper. "I'm caught in the middle of anger, fear, and shame, Dr. Evans. What if they see me differently? What if they don't understand? What if they see it as my fault? I saw my best friend the other day, and I ran. I ran. I've been avoiding her. She tried to stop me from going to that party, and I didn't listen."

Dr. Evans nodded sympathetically. "Those are valid feelings, Ashley. But from what you've told me from our first session, Sara and David care about you deeply. I'm sure they're worried and want to support you. Sometimes, letting others in can be a vulnerable and uncomfortable but a crucial step in the healing process."

Ashley sighed, her shoulders slumping slightly. "I know. Rebecca's been amazing, and I don't know what I would have done without her. But it's still so hard to talk about."

"Rebecca?" Dr. Evans asked, surprised, as this was the first time someone named Rebeca had been mentioned.

"Yeah, I met her not too long ago, and we've kinda clicked. She's a student, and she's helped me open up surprisingly. She was adamant that I tell you."

"Okay. Well, that's a good start. You should consider sharing with Sara and David as well. You don't have to share everything all at once. Maybe start by letting them know you're going through a difficult time and that you appreciate their support. You can share more details when you feel ready."

Ashley nodded slowly, soaking up Dr. Evans' words. "I guess I can try. I just don't want to burden them with my problems."

"You're not a burden, Ashley," Dr. Evans said firmly but kindly. "Friends are there to support each other through the good and the bad. It's okay to lean on them, just as they would lean on you."

A small, hopeful smile appeared on Ashley's face. "I'll try. I'll talk to them." Ashley felt a small glimmer of hope. "Thank you, Dr. Evans, for your advice."

Dr. Evans smiled warmly. "It's wonderful that you have a friend like Rebecca. Having a strong support system is crucial. And remember, you're not alone." Dr. Evans took a pause, gauging the right words to say in the moment. "I also want you to know that I am a licensed counselor who works in the center, and since you're over the age of 18, I don't have to report the rape legally. But, I will if you want me to or if you ever decide to report, I'll walk with you through it."

Ashley nodded and thanked her.

Over the next few weeks, Ashley continued her sessions with Dr. Evans. The counseling helped her navigate her emotions, teaching her coping mechanisms and providing a safe space to express her fears and pain. Slowly, Ashley began to feel a sense of relief and empowerment.

Rebecca remained a constant source of support, always ready with a kind word or a comforting hug, but careful to do so off campus.

Ashley started to open up more, sharing her thoughts and feelings with Rebecca. With each passing day, her feelings for Rebecca grew. Ashley, unsure of these uncharted emotions, had conflicting inner turmoil. She tried to suppress her feelings because it didn't seem natural to her, but the urge to embrace those emotions grew louder and louder until it was the only thing she could hear.

Dr. Evans had asked to meet Ashley one morning, and she wondered why she would call her without an appointment.

Chapter Sixteen

David and Sara strolled through the park with their hands interlocked. It was a quiet afternoon, and the sun cast a warm glow over the campus.

David glanced at Sara, her laughter lighting up her face thanks to the story David had just told her.

"I still can't believe you did that," Sara chuckled, shaking her head.

David grinned. "I was a rebellious kid. What about you? What's the craziest thing you've ever done?"

Sara's smile faded slightly as she thought about her answer. She couldn't think of anything "crazy" that she had done, especially not as a child. She didn't want to appear boring to him, but there was nothing she could think of. "I lied to mom that I was sick, but I was just too tired to go to school! Got grounded for a week, but it was worth it."

David stared at her, weirdly. "That's it?"

"I told a lie!" Her voice rose, defending her answer, assuring him that it was the worst she's done.

They burst out laughing, and for a moment, everything felt

perfect. David had never felt this way about anyone before. His feelings for Sara were intense, but he struggled to find the right words to express them.

As they walked back towards the dorms, David squeezed Sara's hand a little tighter. "I really like spending time with you, Sara. You mean a lot to me."

Sara looked up at him, her eyes sparkling. "I feel the same way."

They stopped by the entrance to Sara's dorm, reluctant to part ways. David leaned in, almost about to kiss her, feeling his heart race, when she pulled away. Sara's cheeks were flushed. Flee from sexual immorality. That was one of the things that stuck with her in Sunday school, and it found the perfect time to interrupt.

"Goodnight, David." She spoke, heading into her dorm building. And hoping to distract from her withdrawal, she added, "I have a game tomorrow, remember, so I have to get up early."

"Goodnight, Sara," David replied, feeling a whole lot of emotions as he watched her go. It wasn't just that he liked her; he was in love with her. But the words stayed lodged in his throat, unspoken.

* * *

Ashley sat in Dr. Evans' office, this time feeling more comfortable—it was indeed different from when she walked in a couple of months ago. The room was quiet; the soft hum of the air conditioner was the only sound. Dr. Evans sat across from her, a kind and patient look in her eyes.

"Ashley, I called you because I have a suggestion to make, and it's really up to you to decide if you feel comfortable doing this or not." Dr. Evans said gently.

Ashley took a deep breath, her mind racing. She wondered what Dr. Evans would suggest. Things have been going so well lately, and she didn't want to mess with what was working.

"Alright, Ashley, I thought about this, and as I mentioned previously, there are resources and people who can support you. Have you considered speaking out about what happened? Sometimes, sharing your story can help others and bring about change."

Ashley was caught off guard by the idea. The idea of sharing her story was something she hadn't thought of because she had just begun sharing with Dr. Evans and Rebecca, but now, to tell others, tears fell down her face. She felt an overwhelming sense of care. The advice that Dr. Evans has given her has helped her to make leaps in her progress. So, for Dr. Evans to mention sharing her story to help her and others sparked determination in her eyes, with a glimpse of fear.

"Maybe—maybe I could. I don't want anyone else to feel the way I did. If speaking out can help one person, it's worth it."

Dr. Evans picked up a folder from her desk and opened it, revealing a list of student NGOs and off-campus support groups.

"Alright, Ashley, there's the Sexual Assault Survivor Support Group. They meet weekly and provide a safe space for survivors to share their experiences and offer each other support. It's a small, confidential group, and many students find it incredibly empowering. What do you think, is that okay with you?" Dr. Evan asked as Ashley nodded.

Dr. Evans continued, "There's also the Women's Resource Center. They offer counseling, legal advice, and advocacy. They can help you navigate the process of reporting the assault and finding legal support if you choose to go that route."

"Thank you, Dr. Evans. Thank you"

* * *

"Hey, Sara," Tory called out. Tory was Sara's classmate and knew how close she was with Ashley. "I'm so sorry about Ashley. I haven't been able to speak to her; I lack the words to tell her," he said, concerned.

"Ashley?" Sara asked. She couldn't understand what Tory was saying, and the fact that she was surprised surprised him!

"You haven't heard about Ashley?" Tory asked, his eyes wide with concern. "She was raped on campus and now she's launched a campaign to raise awareness about rape and campus safety protocols." Sara's jaw clenched, and she stood up from the garden and moved along with Tory to the school courtyard.

David, who had gone to get some snacks, saw her leaving quickly and immediately knew something had gone wrong. "Sara!" He called as he ran to her.

Sara stood in the middle of the bustling campus courtyard, posters and flyers from the rape awareness campaign surrounding them. The atmosphere was electric with conversations, and students moved about, some taking pamphlets, others signing petitions. Sara's mind was reeling from the information she had just learned—her best friend had been raped.

"I can't believe this," David said, his voice strained with emotion.

"I had no idea she was going through that. She went through that all alone." Sara clenched her fists, and a mixture of anger, guilt, and confusion washed over her.

David, noticing the look of hurt on Sara's face, held her hand and moved closer, deciding to attend the rally. Ashley stood on the makeshift stage, a microphone in her hand. She looked nervous but determined.

"Thank you all for being here," Ashley began, her voice steady. "I never imagined I'd be standing here, sharing my story. But I realized that staying silent only helps the perpetrators. We need to speak out, to support each other, and to create a campus where everyone feels safe."

The crowd erupted in applause. David pulled Sara all the way to the front, wanting to be as close to Ashley as possible. When she saw them, her expression didn't soften; it was one of disappointment, but she continued. Sara's eyes filled with tears at the sight of that.

"We're here for you, Ashley," Tory called out, his voice strong.

"Always," people added, giving her a thumbs-up.

Ashley smiled; a mixture of relief and strength washed over her. "Thank you. Your support means everything."

As the rally continued, other students shared their own experiences and voiced their support for Ashley's campaign for a safer campus. It was a powerful moment of unity and resilience. Sara felt a sense of guilt swell within her. This was what love and friendship were about. Standing by each other, no matter what, and she failed at it. After the rally, David and Sara found Ashley sitting on a bench, looking exhausted but content. They sat down beside her, offering their support.

"You were amazing up there," David said, hugging her.

"Yeah, really brave," Sara added.

Ashley nodded, her eyes shining with tears. "Thank you. I couldn't have done it without Dr. Evans and Rebecca. Knowing I have people like them makes all the difference."

Sara lost her mind; she couldn't hold it in any longer. "Oh My God, Ashley!" She shouted. "Having support like them? I'm honestly happy that you have a support system, but I'm totally caught off guard—I've been trying to talk to you and connect with you for weeks! I tried to understand what was going on. I saw you the other day, and you ran. Like, ran as fast as you could to get away from me. You shut us out. And for you to say that—.

The atmosphere was tense, and murmurings from students passing by filled the air. Sara shoved her tears and words back in. It was like a dagger had been forced in her heart, turned, and pushed some more to ensure the damage had been done. Sara didn't understand, but this wasn't about her. This was Ashley's moment. Sara silenced her frustrations.

Ashley crossed her arms, her expression guarded. "Really? Are you trying to act upset? You both made me feel like a burden; you made everything about yourselves. You wanna know something? The day you came to me crying about how jealous you felt and how you were unsure what to do about David, that was the morning after my rape."

Sara's eyes widened as Ashley's demeanor that day made sense now.

"Yeah!" Ashley continued. "But it was all about you! You didn't care!" A stream of tears fell, and her voice broke.

Sara's heart tightened. "Ashley, that's not fair. I reached out to you. I visited your dorm. I called, I texted! For God's sake, you literally ran away from me!"

Ashley cut her off, her voice shaking with anger. "You called. Texted. So, what if I didn't respond? You just assumed I didn't want to be bothered. Did you ever think that maybe I needed you to try harder?"

"Har—." Sara was cut off.

David stepped forward, interjecting with his brow furrowed with concern. "Ashley, we care about you. We had no idea what you were going through."

Ashley turned her gaze and frustration to him. Her eyes filled with hurt. She lashes out, "Of course, you didn't. You were too busy with each other to notice anything else."

"Are you serious right now? All Sara could do was talk about you and if she was doing enough to reach you?" David interjected.

Sara took a deep breath, trying to stay calm. "Ashley, I understand you're hurting, but pushing us away isn't the answer. Let us be there for you now."

Ashley shook her head, tears brimming in her eyes. "It's too late, I don't need you to be here. I don't want pity from you or David. I've found support elsewhere, people who understand." Ashley walked away, leaving Sara and David standing in stunned silence.

Chapter Seventeen

Ashley's hands trembled as she held her phone, staring at the contact list. She hesitated for a moment before tapping on Rebecca's name. "Please pick up," Ashley cried.

"Hey, Ashley. What's up?" Rebecca's voice was warm and familiar, instantly soothing Ashley's frayed nerves.

"Please, can I come over? I, I need someone to talk to," Ashley's voice quivered, barely holding back tears.

"What's wrong?" Rebecca was filled with concern.

"I can tell you when I get there. Which dorms do you stay in? I can be there, I'll be there in like twenty minutes." Ashley replied.

"I'm not on campus," Rebecca said. She was at home, which wasn't far from campus, but was hesitant to have Ashley over, yet she could hear the urgency in Ashley's voice. She thought quickly, "But we can meet at a place that's not too far from campus. I'll send you the address."

Rebecca knew Ashley was running a campaign and had been thinking about her all day. Rebecca had come up with another excuse that Ashley bought. Rebecca didn't want to raise any suspicion with any staff or Ashley in case she had to "switch code."

Just as Rebecca said, the location was close to campus. The walk allowed Ashley to release some of her frustration so she wouldn't bleed hurt all over Rebecca. As Ashley walked into the front doors of the café, she could tell it was a place that wasn't frequented a lot. Besides the young lady working the counter, there was one other person in the corner of the café, with his headphones on, minding his business.

Rebecca waved her hand to get Ashley's attention as she entered. Concern etched on her face as she saw that Ashley had been crying. Rebecca was in a nook of the café, away from the only other patron, so that they could have some privacy. Without a word, Ashley sat down next to Rebecca and lay her head on her shoulder.

"What's wrong, Ashley?" she asked softly, stroking her hair.

"I don't know how to explain it. I feel betrayed. Sara tried to make me feel like I was crazy for being upset and hurt," Ashley trembling between words, her voice cracking. "Everything's a mess."

Rebecca placed her arm around her shoulder; her presence made Ashley feel safe. But there was something else bothering Ashley. Something deeper. While she couldn't put her finger on it, something in her soul craved affection —to belong — but it felt sinister. Something that caused her to have conflicting emotions.

She wasn't sure if the trauma was making her crave it or if it was clouding her judgment. She wasn't sure how to feel towards Rebecca. It was as if her emotions were on a seesaw. One half was reserved in expressing her feelings, perhaps due to shame and uncertainty, but the other half was ready to be engulfed by the wave of affection and safety.

Ashley looked up, eyes filled with tears. "Why do I always feel better with you? You make me feel safe."

Rebecca smiled gently. "Because I care about you, Ashley, more than you know."

There was a shift between them. Something Ashley couldn't put into words, but that made her feel reassured. For a moment, all you could hear was the numbing sound of the ceiling fans in the café.

Something about the sound of the fan and the breeze from it was nostalgic for Ashley. They sat there as all the words that needed to be shared had already been said. The strokes in her hair were good enough for Ashley. The silence was healing—no cheers, no applause, no arguing, just the stillness and the appreciation of this moment.

* * *

On the same morning the rally was taking place on campus, Lewis was appearing before a judge. In the courtroom, he saw his parents, a breath of mercy amid the wave of injustice he was drowning in. Lewis called his parents with his one phone call, and they had hired an attorney within the state to handle Lewis' case.

Given who his parents were, Lewis was released on bail and permitted to return home until the next court date. Given that the alleged crime happened on campus, the university quietly approved Lewis's leave of absence until the case is resolved.

The inside of a courtroom had a new perspective for Lewis. While courtroom stories and litigation were familiar to him through his parents, actually being the subject of one took a toll on him. He had become hardened and changed—like leather that had been left out in the sun for too long.

He sat in his parents' hotel room, the weight of the day pressing down on him. His father, a stern look of determination on his face, paced back and forth while his mother sat beside him, a comforting hand on his shoulder.

"Tell us everything, Lewis," his father urged gently. "We need to know exactly what happened."

Lewis took a deep breath, recounting the events of his wrongful arrest. "I was just jogging on campus when the police stopped me. They said I matched the description of a suspect and wouldn't listen when I told them who I was." He continued his story, without omitting the mention of "you people."

His mother's eyes blazed with anger. "This is unacceptable. They can't treat you like this. You people!"

Lewis nodded, feeling a mix of anger and helplessness. His father clenched his jaw. "This isn't just a misunderstanding. It's racial profiling. Don't worry, we have the best attorney on your case. "

His mother knelt in front of him, her voice softening. "Lewis, we're going to fight this. We'll make sure they know they can't get away with this." Lewis felt a surge of gratitude and resoluteness. They checked out of the hotel and returned home while the attorney they hired handled things.

* * *

Sara sat alone in her dorm room—the silence heavy around her. The guilt and sorrow over her broken friendship with Ashley gnawed on her. She couldn't shake the feeling that maybe she had failed her friend.

She thought about everything Ashley said and began to find meaning in them. Maybe she had been too invested in this relationship that she lost not just her friendship but herself—she barely prayed like she used to, her spiritual life hung by a thread, and everything was going wrong.

One evening, David visited Sara and was trying to talk with her, but she was too invested in studying to pay attention to him. David confronted her, his frustration evident. "Sara, what's going on? You haven't heard a word I said, plus you've been distant lately."

Sara looked up from her book, and her expression was troubled. "David, I feel like I need to find myself again. I've been thinking a lot about everything that's happened, especially with Ashley. I feel like she was right. I lost sight of who I am when I got involved with you."

David's face fell. "Involved with me! What are you saying? That being with me was a mistake?"

Sara shook her head, "No, David. It's just that I've neglected other parts of my life. I wasn't there for Ashley when she needed me. I got so wrapped up in us that I missed the signs."

David frowned, hurt and bewilderment mixed in his eyes. "You can't blame yourself or us for what happened to Ashley! You didn't know, and you tried your best."

"Maybe, but maybe I didn't try hard enough," Sara said softly.

David's expression hardened. He found himself wanting to lash out, but he paused, trying to catch himself. He didn't want to say anything he would regret. "So now what? You're just going to push me away because you feel guilty?"

"I just need some time," Sara explained. "You know the season has officially started, I need to work on my friendship with Ashley, stay on top of my grades, and most importantly, reconnect with my faith. This is who I've always been, and I lost sight of that."

David clenched his jaw, his voice rising in anger. "So, you mean I was just a distraction? Something that pulled you away from your" he air quotes "true self?"

Sara's heart ached at his words. "No, David. You're important to me. I just need some time to clear my head and figure things out—alone."

David stood up, his face a mask of anger and hurt. "If being with me made you lose sight of who you are, then maybe our relationship was a mistake."

Sara's tears spilled over as she watched him walk away. She sat there, prayed for strength, hoping that in time, she could mend her broken friendships and find her way back to herself.

Chapter Eighteen

Almost a week had passed since David and Sara last talked. Sara wondered if she had said the right thing. While she had wanted time alone, it had been days since she had heard from David, and she was having withdrawals and second thoughts.

David felt lost, like a puzzle missing its centerpiece. The days had blended together as if time itself had no desire to move forward. Not being with or talking to Sara left David alone with an overwhelming flood of feelings, and he was drowning. He was lying on his bed when Shawn barged into his room.

David was pissed, "Bruh, what the hell?"

"Relax, bro, you've been lovesick over 'Sister Sara', you need to shake it off, and I'm here to get you out of your funk," Shawn said, throwing a ticket at him.

"Get out. Get out, bruh!" David mustered all of what he could say as if he was taking his last breath before he drowned in his feelings.

"It's tonight at 10 pm. See you there," Shawn said, leaving David's room. David went back, staring at the ceiling before rolling over to look at the ticket. It was a ticket to one of the frat parties on campus. One of the parties that he's been wanting to attend because he's heard some legendary stories about their parties.

He lay there, between the wave of grief pulling him back in and another lulling him towards a night of relief. He thought, *This might actually help me. I need to get my mind off her.*

* * *

David felt a sense of relief as he got to the party. Tired of the emotional distance that had grown between him and Sara, he needed this change of scenery and some fun. The music was loud, the atmosphere lively, and for a while, David let go of his worries and immersed himself in the scene.

As he mingled and enjoyed himself, Emily had been staring at him since he arrived. She was with her girlfriends, and they were gassing her up to talk to him. Her sultry look caught his eye. She was confident and captivating, with an easy smile and an engaging presence.

"He's staring!" One of the girls said, all giddy. "Come on, Emy. Girl, he's fine. He's so into you. Look how he's staring. Go show him what you've got," they all said, cheering her on.

"You all are crazy," Emily laughed. She freshened up her lipstick, stood up, and adjusted her dress. She glided over to David.

"Hi there," she said with a playful grin. "I couldn't help but notice you, and I see you've been staring at me. You got something you want to tell me?"

David smirked, intrigued. "I guess you could say I'm just trying to find something interesting to get into tonight."

"Well," she said, leaning in slightly, "I think I might be able to help with that. I'm pretty good at keeping things interesting."

David raised an eyebrow, a smile tugging at his lips. "Oh? And how do you intend to do that?"

"Why don't we find someplace a bit quieter?" she suggested, her voice dropping to a more intimate tone. "I'm sure we could come up with something that's more than just, you know, interesting."

David's heart sprinted. Am I drunk already? He thought. He felt the spark between them, but he knew it was something temporary; it felt good. "You're pretty direct. I have to admit, it's refreshing," he said.

She laughed softly, her eyes sparkling. "There are so many other things about me you might like when we find a place where it can just be the two of us."

David stared at her intensely. For a moment, he wished she were Sara, yet at the same time, he just wanted to go wherever she was willing to take him.

Emily noticed he was deep in his thoughts. "I'm sorry if I am being too forward, I am just not one to beat around the bush. I know what I want, and right now, it seems like you're exactly what I'm looking for."

David's smile widened. "And what exactly are you looking for?"

"A little adventure," she replied, her gaze locking with his. "A chance to have some fun. Maybe something more if the night takes us there."

David felt a mix of excitement and hesitation. "You certainly know how to make an offer sound tempting."

"Is that a yes?" she asked, her voice teasing yet earnest.

David hesitated for a moment. "Let's just say you've definitely piqued my interest."

She smiled, her eyes twinkling with satisfaction. "Great. Let's see how much of your interest I was able to get then," she said as she held him by the hand, leading the way. David couldn't help but feel the thrill of the unknown. He enjoyed this a little too much. Emily was making him feel so good in all the wrong ways.

David and Emily made their way to a quieter room, away from the throbbing beats of the party. The room was dimly lit, adding to the intimate atmosphere. As soon as the door closed behind them, she turned to him with a seductive smile. "Looks like we're alone," she said, her voice low and sultry.

David nodded, trying to keep his composure. "Yeah, it does."

"So, I didn't get your name," Emily asked as she poured the alcohol on the desk into the cups."

"David." He replied, taking the cup she offered.

"Mmm, Emily, but it can be Emy to you."

David's head began to spin as he had taken more alcohol than he should have. Taking that last shot of alcohol was a mistake he shouldn't have made. He was drinking like he wanted to forget something; well, he did. He walked over to the bed and sat.

"Umm, that was fast," Emy said, smiling, and without hesitation, she began to undress. Her movements are confident and fluid. David watched, feeling a rush of excitement mixed with a pang of guilt as images of Sara flashed through his mind. He tried to shake them off, but they lingered, creating a storm of conflicting emotions.

Once she was fully undressed, she approached him, her eyes locked on his. She guided him to lie on the bed and straddled him, her skin warm against his. The initial thrill of the moment was overshadowed by David's inability to focus. He felt the pressure to perform and maintain his reputation, but his mind was clouded with thoughts of Sara and the emotional disconnect he was trying to escape.

He shifted uncomfortably, trying to block out images of Sara and the emotional turmoil that accompanied them. Despite his efforts, he found himself unable to fully engage. His arousal was lackluster, and the situation only added to his frustration.

Emily noticed his struggle and paused, her expression shifting to one of concern. "Hey, is everything alright?"

David forced a smile, trying to mask his discomfort. "Yeah, it's just been a long day. I'm sorry."

She nodded, "No worries. It happens. Maybe that's why you've got me. You never know, I might be able to help with that," Emily teased.

David, picturing Sara in an intimate setting, ignited a flicker of arousal. He imagined their moments together, which helped him get an erection. However, the fantasy of Sara quickly shifted from tender memories to something darker. The hurt and frustration from their recent distance clouded his thoughts, and he found himself tussling with mixed emotions.

As he tried to align his physical state with his emotions, he realized something unsettling. His affection for Sara had transformed into something more volatile. The heartache he felt had morphed into bitterness, and his imagination shifted to a more spirited, vengeful fantasy.

He pictured a raw, intense encounter with Sara, one filled with anger and raw desire. The fantasy of dominating her, of reclaiming control, emerged from his frustration. It wasn't what he had ever imagined with her, but in that heated moment, his thoughts were consumed by a need to confront and release his bottled-up emotions.

David's gaze was still on Emily, but all he saw was Sara's face, her betrayal still fresh in his mind. "Maybe you can," he muttered.

The night blurred as they got more intimate. Emily kissed him; she tasted like alcohol, and he didn't hesitate to return the kiss, their kisses growing more urgent. David stood from the bed, pushing Emily against the wall, his hands roaming her body with a desperate need.

"Sara," he groaned, his breath hot against her neck.

"It's Emy," she gasped, trying to bring him back to the present. But David was too far gone, lost in a mix of anger and desire.

He lifted her back onto the bed, his clothes discarded in a frenzy. As they moved together, David's mind was a whirlwind of Sara's face, her laughter, and the hurt she had caused him. "Sara," he moaned again, his voice breaking with a mix of pleasure and pain.

Emily's nails dug into his back; he was being really rough with her, but he hardly noticed, consumed by his need to forget, to replace the hurt with something physical. Their bodies collided in a fierce rhythm, each thrust a desperate attempt to bury his emotions. When it was over, David collapsed beside Emily, his chest heaving. He turned to look at her, but all he could see in his drunken state was the ghost of Sara, still haunting him.

"David," Emily said softly, reaching out to touch his face. "You know I'm not her."

"I know," he replied, his voice hollow. "But I needed you to be," he replied, staring into her eyes.

"I will be whatever you want me to be, but just for tonight," Emily said as she smiled. He pulled her to himself, their bodies rubbing against each other as they fell asleep.

The harsh morning light pierced through the blinds. As David awoke, his head was pounding with the remnants of last night's alcohol. He grumbled, covering his eyes as he turned to the side. The space beside him was vacant, the sheets still warm but devoid of Emily's presence.

"Emy?" he called out weakly, but the only response was the emptiness he felt, which spoke louder than words ever could.

He forced himself to sit up, his body protesting with every movement. He glanced around, spotting his phone on the nightstand. The screen lit up with numerous missed calls and messages—all from Sara.

Regret surged through him as he picked up the phone and scrolled through the missed calls list. His voicemail was full, and the last message was from Sara; her voice trembled with worry.

"David, please call me back. I need to talk to you. I'm so sorry, you misunderstood what I said. Call me back, please."

He let the phone drop onto the bed, rubbing his head in frustration. The events of the previous night flooded back; the bar, Emily's touch, and the way he had moaned Sara's name, embarrassment and regret twisted his stomach.

He stumbled to the bathroom, as he sprinkled cold water on his face, trying to wash away the leftover of his drunken state. His reflection stared back at him, hollow-eyed and weary. The man looking back seemed like a stranger, someone consumed by pain and anger.

He returned to the bedroom, glancing at the rumpled sheets, and couldn't help but feel a wave of self-loathing. He had used Emily as a stand-in for Sara, trying to erase the hurt through a fleeting moment of physical connection. But it didn't work. The pain was still there, gnawing at him.

David sat back on the edge of the bed, the phone clutched in his hand. Not wanting to face the reality of his situation. But for now, all he could do was sit in the aftermath of his choices.

Chapter Nineteen

It's been some time since Ashley gave her speech. Before, she was known for her sociable demeanor. But now, she had become known for something else: her courage in speaking out about her own experience with rape. While Ashley was nervous and her hands shook as she held the microphone that day, her voice remained steady because she no longer wanted to give her power away. That day, she had found what was lost—her voice. In the weeks following, Ashley noticed a shift. Women she barely knew began to approach her, sharing their stories, seeking solace, and finding strength in her courage.

Racheal, a beautiful young lady who had been battling with the same trauma, was challenged when she heard her speech. She felt that if Ashley could do it, then she could too. Flashbacks of Ashley's speech kept coming to her.

"I stand here today to share my story. It's not an easy one to tell, but I believe it's necessary. A few months ago, I was raped. It happened on this very campus, a place where I should feel safe.

(There are gasps from the audience. Ashley takes a deep breath.)

I felt embarrassed, scared, and alone. But I am not alone. Many of you here have faced similar horrors. We need to create a space where we can talk about these experiences openly, without fear of judgment or punishment."

Rachael's flashback was interrupted when she decided she was going to join Ashley in her quest to create a safe space on campus.

Ashley was sitting alone in the campus cafeteria, eating her lunch, wishing Rebecca could join her, but Rebecca had to take a rain check. Ashley couldn't understand why Rebecca seemed more distant lately, but didn't think too much about it because Ashley hadn't had that much downtime. Rachael approached nervously while Ashley was still lost in her thoughts.

"Hi, Ashley, right?" Rachael asked, trying to break a smile.

"Yes, that's me. And you are?" Ashley asked, smiling right back at her.

"I'm Rachael, Rachael Acevedo. I heard your speech a few weeks ago. It was courageous. I wanted to thank you."

"Thank you for saying that. It means a lot," Ashley replied softly.

"I, I have a story too. It happened off-campus, but I haven't been able to talk about it. Not until I heard you," Racheal said hesitantly.

Reaching out to hold Racheal's hand, Ashley offered solace and said, "You're not alone, Rachael. I'm here to listen."

Rachael smiled at her, "I would like to join you in creating a space where more of us can share our stories. So that no one feels alone, like I did. Like you were."

Rachael's words were like a balm, healing her from the same fire that had burned them. While other women had shared their stories with Ashley, turning her into a bridge to help them leave behind their shame. Rachael was the only one who said she wanted to walk beside Ashley in this journey. While there were other support groups on campus, and Ashley managed to attend a few, something was still missing. And that something is what compelled Ashley to start her group. Racheal's words had become a relief.

Ashley insisted that Racheal sit down and join her. They talked for a while, getting to know each other—learning more about Ashley's vision —and put together a plan.

* * *

Ashley and Rachael put it up in a blog and social media pages, and in just a few days, a lot of ladies had signed up. The following week, Ashley was standing at the front of a room. About a dozen women were seated in a circle, some looking nervous, others resolute.

"Thank you all for coming. Welcome to our first meeting. I want this to be a safe space where we can talk openly about our experiences and support one another." Ashley said, for a moment, she couldn't believe she was doing this. She's come a long way from silently sitting in Dr. Evans's office.

A young lady named Miriam speaks up. "I was assaulted by someone I thought was my friend. For the longest time, I blamed myself. But hearing you, Ashley, made me realize it wasn't my fault. None of it was," Miriam said as a murmur of agreement passed through the group.

"Thank you for sharing that, Miriam. It's so important to remember that it's never our fault. We did nothing wrong."

Sarah, another young lady in their midst, raises her hand. "I was raped at a party. I didn't know who to turn to. The police were no help. They just asked me what I was wearing, how much I'd had to drink. The police," she pauses. "The system failed us, and that's why we're here. To support each other and do what they are unable to."

Rachael, from the cafeteria, speaks up. "I want to help. I don't want to share my story; I want to make a difference. I want to advocate for change. Some policy changes on campus. Organize more awareness events, but with training, educate people about consent and respect."

"That's a fantastic idea, Rachael. Together, we can make a difference. This group is just the beginning," Ashley said, smiling and feeling a surge of hope.

The group stayed true to their word and, in a matter of weeks, organized an awareness event with on-site training workshops and demonstrations. There were banners, pamphlets, and a stage set up. Ashley steps up to the microphone.

"Thank you all for being here. This event is about more than just raising awareness; it's about creating change. We are survivors, and we will not be silenced. We will educate, we will support, and we will fight for a safer campus and policy change."

The crowd cheers, a sense of unity and strength filling the air. Sara smiled from the crowd. She was so proud of Ashley, and even if they weren't cool at the moment, she loved how strong she had become. She had tried reaching out to Ashley, but to no avail. She didn't want to push it. She just wanted to show up and support.

After leaving the event, Sara walked across campus, her thoughts swirling as if they were leaves in an autumn breeze. It seemed like things were worse. Ashley was getting along fine without her. She had found her voice, support, and new friends. David hadn't returned any of her phone calls. She didn't mean to push him away; she just needed some alone time to try to figure things out. She just wished he could understand where she was coming from. Not to mention the balancing act between softball and studying was a teeter-totter that was making her feel queasy.

And just as the wind blows in any direction it chooses, she found her footsteps carrying her near the library—a place where she welcomed its silence as if the silence understood her better than people ever had. As she entered the doors, she saw the shape of her heartbreak standing before her.

Sara approached David, who was talking to his study group. He saw Sara coming, and his expression changed from relaxed to angry. He was hurt by her and angry with himself. He couldn't look her in the eyes. He still felt stained by the memory of what he'd done. Her presence made him ache for a do-over he didn't believe he deserved.

"David, can we talk for a minute?" she asked, guiding him away from his friends for a bit of privacy.

David sighs, "What's there to talk about, Sara?"

"Please, David. I just want to understand what's happening."

David burst out laughing bitterly, "What's happening? Look, Sister Sara, you shouldn't be messing with a sinner like me. Go find someone who fits your perfect little world." He had never called her Sister Sara; those were Shawn's words. But the words flowed out so smoothly as if Hurt had borrowed his voice and spoke recklessly.

Sara felt a dagger in her chest at his words as she replied, "David, that's not fair. I care about you. I never meant to say you were a distraction; that wasn't what I meant at all."

Cutting her off. "Maybe you were not wrong. Maybe I was actually not the right one for you. Just let it go." David dismissed her and her feelings as he turned his back and walked away.

Stunned—as if she had been erased from a picture she belonged in. She stood there for a brief moment until her legs began to feel the weight of her broken heart. She grabbed onto a bookshelf to regain her composure before she walked away.

* * *

Sara sat on her bed, staring at her Bible. She wondered if this was the cross she had to carry, everyone had left her and her efforts to mend her relationships were not yielding at all. She remembered her father's sermons on Matthew 7 about walking the narrow path. Sometimes doing things God's way may seem difficult, lonely and quite frankly you may not understand. But if you trust God and his timing, your obedience will bear fruit.

Everything seemed to be spiraling. Sarah had never experienced this type of situation and she was doubting if she was doing things 'God's way'. Her roommate, Jess, entered her room to ask to borrow something when she noticed tears flowing down her cheeks and Sara's bleak stare at the wall. "Hey, Sara, what's wrong?"

Sara was startled as she didn't realize anyone else was in the room. Jess and Sara were pretty good roommates, as they were both from small towns and shared the same faith. "Everything's falling apart, Jess," she replied as she wiped the tears away from her face as if it were to erase what Jess had already seen.

Jess had assumed something was off with Sara, but she wasn't sure, plus she had heard David leave their dorm angrily weeks ago. "I'm so sorry, Sara. What's going on?" Jess said, sitting beside her, trying to console her. Not sure of the right words to say.

"I don't understand. One minute, everything was fine. And now —it's like I'm the bad person."

"Sometimes people change, and it's not your fault. Maybe he's just in his feelings and might be going through something else he's not ready to talk about."

"It feels like everything in my life is crumbling. Not just David— everything." Sara cried, running her hand through her hair. "My friendship with Ashley, I can barely concentrate in class or at a game, everything just seems off. I feel so lost."

"It's okay to feel lost, Sara. But you're not alone. Remember Isaiah 41:10, 'I am with you; do not be dismayed, for I am your God.'" She paused and took a look at her, "And if things get too bad, it's pretty much the end of the school year, so you can just leave it all behind you," she joked, trying to lighten the situation.

Sara leaned into Jess, grateful for her support. She knew she needed the word of God to strengthen her, but at that moment, she allowed herself to feel.

* * *

Lewis sat in the courtroom, his heart pounding. His father had taken the case to court just like he promised; he had sued the police for harassment and profiling. Lewis glanced around at the spectators, reporters, and a few familiar faces from campus.

The police had also placed charges against Lewis for resisting arrest during his jog, and it had sparked outrage. Many saw it as a clear case of racial profiling. Lewis felt the weight of it all pressing down on him. He was angry and bitter, deeply feeling the sting of injustice.

After a long morning in court, recess was called. Lewis stepped out into the hallway as his phone rang. It was Sara calling to check in on him. She had called him a few weeks ago and learned about his ordeal. Even though what Lewis was going through had nothing to do with Sara, she felt guilty, and it reassured her even more of how 'bad' a friend she had been.

"Lewis, hey. I wanted to see how you're holding up," Sara said, concerned.

"How do you think I'm holding up, Sara? This whole thing is a joke," Lewis spewed bitterly.

"I know it's not fair. What happened to you was wrong, and it should never have happened."

"It's not just this. It's everything. This country, this system. It's all rigged against us."

"I can't imagine how you feel, but I want you to know that not everyone is like that. There are people who care, who want to help."

"Like who? The police? The justice system? They don't care about us. If they do, we shouldn't be going back and forth like this; it is clear what this is. They're trying to sweep it under the rug. Screw them, man." Lewis had allowed his anger and frustration to speak for him.

"No, not them. But people like me. And others who are fighting for justice. We're here for you, Lewis."

"It's hard to see that right now. All I feel is anger."

"I get that. And it's okay to be angry. But don't let it consume you. There's more to this world than hate."

Lewis couldn't help but struggle with his emotions.

"Can I offer you a prayer, Lewis? I know it might not seem like much, but sometimes it helps to have a little faith."

"Sure, I guess. It can't hurt."

"Dear God, please give Lewis strength and peace. Please help him to see that he is not alone. That there are people who care about him and support him. And above all, that You love him. Heal his heart and guide him through this difficult time. Amen."

"Amen. You wearing your papa's mantle?" Lewis joked.

"Shut up," Sara replied as they laughed. It felt good to laugh as she hadn't done so in some time.

"Hey, how are David and Ashley? I miss you all, man."

"They are good," Sara replied, not wanting to add to Lewis' burden. During her call with Lewis a few weeks ago, she never brought up what was going on between the three. After she heard what happened to him, she wanted the focus to stay on him.

"That's all? You okay?" Lewis asked, concerned.

"Yes," Sara said, smiling through her teeth, but underneath was a heart full of hurt and sorrow, crying out to be consoled and mended.

"Well, okay. Thanks for the prayer, Sara."

"Anytime. And you're not going through this alone. We're all here for you."

"It's hard not to feel isolated. Like no one really understands."

"I might not understand completely, but I'm here to listen. And so are a lot of other people."

"I've just seen so much ugliness in this situation. It's hard to believe there's any good left."

"There are some good people left. You are one of them. Don't allow this situation to dim your light."

"You really believe that?" His heart felt lighter.

"I do. And I believe in you, Lewis. You're stronger than you know."

"Thanks, Sara. I appreciate it and you."

"Anytime. I'm here for you."

They ended the call. Lewis was focused and taking in all that Sara had just said when Kourtney sat beside him.

"Hey, I thought you might need some company."

"Yeah, that would be nice," Lewis said, smiling slightly. He had apologized for not listening to her when she spoke to him about situations like this before.

"No biggie, but how are you feeling?" Kourtney asked.

"A bit better. Talking helps. I just spoke to a friend, and knowing I have you all's support makes a difference."

"Good. You'll get through this, Lewis. One step at a time."

"Yeah, one step at a time."

The break was over, and the trial continued. Lewis's anger and bitterness were still there, but they were tempered by the hope and kindness he saw in people like Kourtney and Sara. He realized that while the fight against racism was far from over, he didn't have to fight it alone. Together, they could make a difference, one step at a time.

Sara felt better after speaking to Lewis. It felt good to be there for him and pray for him. It almost felt redemptive. As she finished writing in her journal, she realized that all she was going through was a phase and everything would get better—hopefully soon. She prayed, closed her journal, and took a deep breath, feeling a bit lighter. She stood up and had a slight smile on her face as if she was telling the world that she was ready to face whatever came next.

Sara's words whispered back at her, 'You are stronger than you know' and 'You aren't going through this alone'. It was as if God were ministering to her, reminding her that the same message of hope you gave Lewis also applied to her.

While Sara felt slightly refreshed, David was clinging to the pieces of what was. He was trying his best to forget Sara, but her absence gnawed at him. He replayed all that transpired that day at the library. Since their 'separation', he had been burying his pain in parties and weed. While it was supposed to be a temporary escape, the habit was lingering like a bad date that didn't get the hint that this wasn't going to work. His behavior was taking a toll on him. His grades were slipping, and his performance on the basketball team was suffering.

David sat in his bed, in a dimly lit room, music pounding in his headphones. He took a long drag from a blunt, blew it out of the opening of the window in his room, and took a sip from his red cup.

While he had placed a towel under the door to prevent the smoke from exiting his room, he forgot to lock his bedroom door.

With the music blasting loudly in his ear and his eyes closed, he didn't hear his teammate enter his room.

"Hey, man, you've been going hard lately. Everything okay?" Chris asked.

"Yeah, just blowing off some steam. No big deal." David said, forcing a smile, but his eyes barely opened.

"Man, you need to straighten up."

"Stopping stressing. I got this."

"Uh, no, you don't. Man, things aren't looking good for you, and here you are smoking weed. You've been slipping. Don't be surprised if someone else gets your spot on the team."

"They wish," he smirked.

"Aiight, man. Don't forget we got practice tomorrow. Coach is already on your case."

"I know, I know. I'll be there."

Chris gave him a concerned look but nodded. David took another drag, trying to numb the ache inside.

* * *

David stumbled onto the court, his eyes bloodshot and his movements sluggish. Coach Johnson watched him with a frown.

"David, you look like hell. What's going on?"

"Just a rough night, Coach. I'm fine."

"Fine? Your performance says otherwise. Get it together, or you're off the team."

"I'll do better, Coach. Promise," David sighed.

"I hope so. We need you at your best, not this."

David nodded as he felt the weight of his coach's disappointment and a night of bad decision-making.

After practice, David decided to take the shortcut to his dorm by walking through the library. Sara was inside studying when she saw

David walk in, looking disheveled. She approached him cautiously. "David, can we talk?"

"What's there to talk about, Sara?" David responded irritably.

"I'm worried about you. I know we haven't talked in quite some time, but you've changed. Your teammate told me he is concerned about you—and some of the activities you've been into lately. That isn't you," Sara said, trying to keep her voice low, not to attract any attention.

"You don't know me, Sara. Not anymore."

"I know you're hurting. But this isn't the way to deal with it."

"You think you know everything, don't you? Just leave me alone."

Sara watched him walk away, feeling a deep sadness. She wished she could help him, but she knew he had to want to help himself first. Her father would say, "You can want it more than them, but you aren't able to do it for them. They have to want help for themselves."

David sat on his bed, surrounded by empty cans and half-smoked joints. He stared at his textbooks, knowing he was falling behind.

Get it together, David. You can't keep doing this. He tells himself. He picked up a textbook and tried to study, but his mind kept wandering back to Sara. *Why is it hard for me to say what I want to say? Why do I care so much? I didn't even know I could feel like this, but it hurts.* Frustrated and overwhelmed by his thoughts that weren't getting him anywhere, he threw the book across the room and buried his head in his hands.

He felt suffocated—a pain in his chest. He needed fresh air, and he wasn't getting it in his room. He stood from the bed, gathered his gym bag, and went for a walk. While the campus basketball court was closed. The court off campus was open 24/7. It was a spot some of the guys would go to for extra practice. There were a few people on the court, but they left not too long after his arrival.

Alone on the court, he dribbled, ran drills, and took shots for hours. He was fighting through his emotions. Tired and breathless, he took a deep breath and shot. The ball swished through the hoop as his body went limp, and he fell to the ground.

Chapter Twenty

Ashley was exhausted after meeting with the various organizations interested in working with her. It had been a long day, filled with intense discussions and planning sessions. She was so tired she just needed to unwind, somewhere away from all the busyness, and she decided to visit Rebecca.

She called Rebecca, and Rebecca agreed to let her come over to her place. Rebecca wasn't sure why the word 'yes' flowed so easily from her mouth, but whatever the reason, it was out there now, and Ashley was on her way.

"Hey, come on in," Rebecca greeted her with a warm smile.

"Thanks," Ashley replied, stepping inside and glancing around. She was impressed with Rebecca's apartment. Ashley loved the décor, the ambience, and the arrangement of everything. "I really love your place. Nice. This is too nice for a dorm room," she laughed.

Rebecca tensed; she had rushed to clear her table and everything that might expose her as not a student.

"Yeah, I just prefer it here. It's quieter, and I can focus better."

Ashley nodded. "Makes sense. I'm just so tired from all the meetings and finals." Ashley said grumbling as she sat on her couch.

Rebecca sat down next to Ashley. "What you're doing takes a lot of work, and you're doing an amazing job, Ashley. It took courage to stand up after what you have been through. And not only have you told your story, but you have helped many young women do the same. You started an organization and are building something that will last. You're a brave and special soul."

Ashley blushed slightly, "Thanks, Rebecca. It wouldn't have been possible if it weren't for you and Dr. Evans."

Rebecca tensed up slightly at hearing Dr. Evans' name. It reminded her of the dangerous line between curiosity and consequence she was crossing.

"We didn't do anything. You did all the work, and I'm proud of you," Rebecca said, placing a hand on Ashley's. "And I really admire you for it." The touch lingered, and before Ashley knew it, she had leaned in, but a timer went off, and Rebecca had stood up just in the nick of time to save Ashley from embarrassment. As the timer went off, so did Ashley's illusion that this was something more.

"Oh, I was making something to eat. You are welcome to have some. I made more than enough."

"Thanks. I could eat something," Ashley shook that moment off and enjoyed the meal with Rebecca. She enjoyed herself so much that she didn't realize how late it had gotten. Rebecca encouraged her to stay the night as she could sleep in the guest bedroom. Ashley took her up on the offer and bid her goodnight. Ashley was exhausted, so she went straight to bed.

Ashley woke up as the sun's rays began to peek through the curtains. The bed was very comfortable, definitely an upgrade from the one in her dorm room. She yawned, stretched, and was about to get out of bed when she scanned the room —something caught her eye: a picture on the desk.

While Rebecca was in the picture, someone else caught her eye. She stood and walked closer to the picture to get a better look. Given that she was across the room, she had to be mistaken. She wanted to be mistaken.

But as she stood there, feet away from the image, Ashley's heart sank as she saw the picture.

Ashley felt a surge of anger and betrayal. It was him. The villain that started this horror saga—the face she longed not to see.

Ashley started sobbing, "No, no, no, no. Why?" The shrill of Ashley's cries woke Rebecca, who came running into the guest bedroom.

"Ashley, what's going on?" Rebecca asked, her voice still groggy from sleep.

Ashley slowly turned around as if fear had taken hold of her body. "Who is that?"

"Who, who is what?" Trying to figure out who Ashley is referring to, as she hasn't had her morning cup of coffee, so her brain can begin processing things.

"Who is that—that," pointing at his image now, "in the picture with you?"

"That's my brother. What does this have to do with anything?"

Ashley sobbed in disbelief, grabbed her shoes, and began walking out of the room.

Rebecca tried to slow her down. "Whoa, whoa, whoa, what's going on, Ashley? Just talk to me."

"Well, what you would call a brother is what I would call the worst night of my life."

"What?" Rebecca, still not catching on.

"Your brother raped me."

Those words did more for Rebecca than any cup of coffee could. "What do you mean, my brother raped you? He doesn't even go to this college."

"So, you're calling me a liar?"

"No, perhaps mista—"

Rebecca's words fell flat as her memory flooded her thoughts and froze mid-word, but it was too late. Ashley figured out what she was going to say. Rebecca tried to stop her from leaving, but Ashley was halfway out the door when Rebecca came to. Rebecca remembered that he came to visit that weekend. He didn't stay the length of time he initially said he would. He left suddenly, stating that he had to go help out a friend, and Rebecca didn't think anything of it.

* * *

Parents' Day had arrived — that weekend after finals when the campus came alive again with moving trucks, hugs, and the sound of parents pretending not to pry. It was a chance for them to see what their kids had been up to before packing up for summer break. Most families lingered through Friday's events, then slipped out by Saturday morning. The Day was primarily for first-year students, as they were required to live on campus. A day intended to be full of pride and celebration had quickly descended into a whirlwind of confusion and distress for Sara, Ashley, and David.

Sara hoped she wouldn't say anything that would trigger her parents' concern. Sara's mom was pretty discerning, so Sara wanted to maintain her cool and not give anything away. Her parents didn't know about David, and she wanted to keep it that way. They knew that Ashley and she were friends in the same dorm building, but had no clue their friendship was falling apart.

Ashley was battling with the truth she had just found out, and the last person she wanted to

see at the moment was her mom. She couldn't take any more drama, and her mom was known for drama. Ashley crossed her fingers that her mom would change her mind and not show up.

David just wanted to soothe his troubles with smoking; he didn't care to be bothered by anyone. Frankly, he was tired of caring, as he seemed to be a disappointment to everyone. He knew his parents would show. His parents were committed to him having a good education. They worked hard to send him to a great school so he could get an education and a college basketball scholarship. David didn't want to see his strict dad sober; he felt like a disappointment already, and he didn't want anyone reminding him. So he smoked his blunt to mellow his anxiety.

They all felt a profound sense of loneliness despite the bustling activities around them.

John and Elaine arrived, and Sara greeted them with a hopeful smile. She showed them around, and they even had lunch on campus. She told them excitedly about school, her grades, and even how she started a Bible study with some of the girls on her team. Her parents were proud of her. Proud to see that she still had her faith.

Even with their approval, it didn't cheer Sara up much. She was smiling on the outside, but inside were swelling storm clouds waiting for a downpour.

Ashley was wrestling with her own turmoil. She felt stupid for allowing Rebecca to get that close to her. The betrayal left her reeling, and her mind started to spiral. Did she know? Was she using me to make up for what her brother did? She had to push those feelings aside as she braced herself for her mother's arrival. Her anxiety peaked when she saw her mother stumbling through the campus, clearly intoxicated.

"Hey, Ash! Where are all the hot guys and the party?" her mother slurred, drawing unwanted attention from nearby students and parents.

Ashley's blood was boiling with a mix of embarrassment and anger. "Mom, can you please stop? This isn't the time or place."

Ashley tried to make her keep it down, since people were already watching, but she kept talking, talking down to Ashley. Ashley managed to subdue her mother and bring her into her dorm room, in the hope of saving face.

"Stop being such a pussy, Ashley," her mother snapped, her voice loud and unfiltered.

Ashley's frustration boiled over. "That's enough, Mom! Come on! I'm really not okay! I am trying to survive here all on my own?" she shouted, her voice breaking under the weight of her emotions.

"What the hell is wrong with you?"

Overwhelmed, overstimulated, and just over it, she yelled, "I was raped, Mom." She was shocked that she opened up to her mom. Perhaps it was the longing desire to be vulnerable and have someone understand what she had gone through—something she had with Rebecca.

Her mother's expression briefly shifted to shock, but then she sneered. "Who in the world would want to rape you?"

The nasty words hit Ashley like a physical blow. Tears streamed down her face as she struggled to hold back her sobs. "You never cared, did you? You never listen!" she cried, her voice trembled with anguish.

The argument escalated as their harsh words echoed across the dorm floor. Feeling overwhelmed and desperate for emotional support, Ashley fled, not knowing where to turn. She had pushed Sara away so she would be the last person she would want to see. Her mind raced as she ran, ran with tears blurring her vision and no destination in sight but the desire to be as far away from her mom as possible.

On the other hand, David's parents had arrived and immediately noticed something was off with their son. They tried to talk to David, but they had a hard time getting any information out of him. His father figured he knew who would have some answers if David didn't. Concerned, David's father decided to speak with the coach to see if he knew what was happening with his son.

"Coach, I need to know what's going on with David," David's father asked, his voice tinged with worry.

The coach sighed heavily. "David's been struggling lately. His performance has been slipping, and he's on the verge of being kicked off the team."

David's father felt a sinking feeling in his chest. "What do you mean he's on the verge of being kicked off? How did this happen?"

The coach rubbed his temples. "He's been missing practices, showing up late, and his attitude has been problematic. It's been hard to get through to him. A few days ago, he was found passed out at a basketball court."

David's father nodded grimly, thanked the coach, and sought out his son. He found David and his mom sitting on a bench. David looked distant.

"David, we need to talk," his father said, his tone firm but concerned.

David looked up, his gaze blank. "What's up?"

"Excuse me?" His father was about to discipline David with his hands, but he didn't want to lose focus. "You've been struggling, and I need to know what's going on," his father said, his frustration evident. "You're on the verge of being kicked off the team. Do you understand that?"

David's eyes glazed over as he processed the words. His mind was far from the conversation, preoccupied with thoughts of his next blunt. "Yeah, I get it," he mumbled, not really engaging with his father's concerns.

"David, this isn't just about the team," his father continued. "You're letting everything slip away, and it's affecting your future. You need to get your act together."

David's father's words were a distant hum to him. His thoughts were already drifting to how he'd escape the current mess; the only thing he had in mind was him getting high to numb all the pain.

"You don't understand, Dad," David said, his voice lacking conviction. "I just need a break."

His father's frustration grew. "A break? Apparently, you've been on break all semester. You're about to lose everything you've worked for. You need to face this head-on."

David stared at his father without really seeing him. He knew that he wouldn't even try to understand him. So instead of continuing to explain, he said, "Okay, I'll try."

David's father left, exasperated but hopeful that his son might snap out of it. David, however, remained in his daze, his mind far from the reality of his situation. Feeling the tension between the two, David's mom kissed him on the forehead, told him they would be back in the morning, and went after his father.

Chapter Twenty-One

L ewis' parents built their careers believing that the law could fix things and that truth once revealed, had weight, but they've seen their share of how things can turn unfair for the victim. And this case was turning into one of those times.

The evidence was nearly nonexistent, the claims were buried in policies and fine print, and the county's attorneys hid behind qualified immunity as if it were gospel. Every session felt more like a TV show performance and less like justice being pursued. The judge recommended diverting the case to Alternative Dispute Resolution.

On top of all of that, mocking what Lewis had gone through came the news clip. Privileged student cries racism. The media was playing it on every platform, and Lewis's lawyer had sent it to them as a caution that the public had chosen its side.

After months of holding it in and pursuing justice, Lewis went silent. He allowed his anger to speak for him. With each update came a wound that left him hardened and numb. So when the phone rang and on the other end was the mediator with the offer — dismissal with prejudice, a written apology, and a promise to "review policies"

— there was a long silence in the room. Looks were exchanged, and without words, they were all in agreement.

Lewis's mother finally said, "Let's end this." It wasn't justice. But it was a start — a step toward healing what the system had broken between them.

After the ordeal was finally over, Lewis decided to tell his parents he was changing majors. He would now pursue law. At first, his mom was hesitant; she knew how much Lewis loved engineering and sports, and that this new desire was born of pain.

"Trust me, Mom," Lewis said, holding his mother's hand and almost whispering.

"Law? You know, I have no issues with your choice of majors, but why would you let this experience deter you from what you love? What about your desire for engineering? What about sports? Are you going to throw that all away?"

"That one experience for me was someone's last, Mom. A lot of other black people have and will be harassed by them, and guess what? All they would get is a freaking apology with no real change."

Lewis's mother looked to her husband for help, but he looked away. It was apparent that even if he wasn't in full support, he was going to allow his son to do what he felt was best for himself as long as it wasn't a bad thing.

"Alright." She raised her hands as a sign of surrender.

"So, where do you plan to go?"

"UGA&T."

"Athens?"

"Yes, Mom. They specialize in law and science. I would be able to do well over there," he said confidently as his mom nodded. Whether or not his parents were on board, Lewis was determined to be an advocate for others and serve justice in a broken system.

Lewis's wrongful arrest had set him on a path he never anticipated, but one that would make a difference. It was a path that would bring justice where there was none, and fairness where it was long overdue.

With the trail being drawn out, the end of the school year was near. Lewis wanted to start school right away, so he submitted his paperwork to begin in the summer.

* * *

David's vision blurred as he stumbled through the crowded party. The music was deafening, the room spinning around him. He had lost count of the number of drinks he'd had. Even though the semester was over, he still felt like he was trying to outrun his hurts, disappointments, and sorrow, but it was a race he was losing.

"Yo!"

David had bumped into someone, spilling his glass of alcohol. "Sorry," he mumbled, not able to see clearly. Suddenly, the room tilted violently, and David felt himself falling. He hit the floor hard, his head swimming. Voices around him grew distant, like he was underwater. Then everything went black.

David's head pounded as he squinted against the harsh fluorescent lights of the hospital room. The last thing he remembered was downing another shot at the party. Now, his body felt like it had been wrung out, his throat parched and raw. He tried to sit up, but a wave of nausea pushed him back down.

A nurse entered the room and checked his vitals. "How are you feeling, David?" she asked gently.

"Like hell," he croaked.

"That's to be expected," she replied, adjusting his IV. "You have alcohol poisoning. It's a good thing your friends called 911 when they did."

David's mind raced. His coach, his team, and his mom, he had let everyone down. Panic began to set in as he heard familiar voices outside the door. It was his parents. *Bad news sure does spread quickly*, he thought. The nurse stepped aside as they rushed in, their faces etched with worry and disappointment.

"David, what were you thinking?" his mother asked, her voice trembling.

"I don't know, Mom," he mumbled, unable to meet her eyes.

His father stood with his arms crossed, his expression a mixture of anger and concern. "You do not ever know, do you?" David's mom glared at her husband, signaling that this isn't the time. "This is unacceptable, David. You've jeopardized your future, your health. The school has been in touch. They're talking about suspension and losing your scholarship." His father continued, unmindful of the look his wife gave him.

David's heart sank. Hearing those words from his father somehow made it real. He had worked so hard to get a scholarship to play on the university's basketball team. He wanted to get well, but it's like he couldn't get a grip and everything had slipped through his fingers.

"Can I be alone?" He asked, his dad almost losing it, but was interrupted by the nurse who walked in.

"Please, sir, you may leave now," the nurse said, overhearing the conversation and noticing an increased heart rate on the monitor. David's mother pulled her husband's arm, signaling to leave, to avoid causing a scene.

David asked the nurse when he could leave. She explained that his liver enzymes were elevated, so they are monitoring him until everything normalizes.

The next morning, his coach arrived. Coach was a stern man, but he had always believed in David's potential. Today, however, his expression was grimly resolved.

"David," he began, "I'm sorry, but you know the rules. I can't help it. I have to kick you off the team. I fought for you, but you need to get your life back on track. This is a wake-up call. Focus on your recovery. Since it's the end of the year, you'll have to sit out a semester. And if you want back on this team, you have to earn it. Clean record, 3.0 GPA, drug tests every month. You miss one and you're done, and I can't guarantee a scholarship."

David nodded, swallowing hard. "I understand, Coach." As the coach left, David felt a sense of loss greater than he had ever known. Basketball was his life, his identity. Without it, who was he? He didn't come from money like Lewis. It was his skills on the court that landed him in one of the best high schools. He didn't even stay in the same county as the school. His parents saved what they could for college, but they relied on his abilities and decent grades to secure him a college scholarship.

David distracted himself from wallowing in his pity by watching television. A knock at the door caught his attention. He looked up to see Sara. Her eyes were red as if she had been crying all night.

"David," she said softly, stepping into the room. "Are you okay?"

David's heart ached; he wanted to run into her embrace, but at the same time, he felt this was her fault; she turned him into this. Now, looking at her, all he could feel was anger and shame, even as he wanted to tell her everything —to confess his love —the words stuck in his throat. Instead, anger and frustration bubbled up.

"I'm fine, Sara. And you didn't have to come," he snapped.

Sara shook her head, but was not surprised. "I wanted to make sure you were okay. I care about you and you know that."

"Care," he scoffed, turning away. "Pity is not care, Sara."

"David, what's going on?" she asked, her voice breaking. "Why are you pushing me away?"

"Because you deserve better!" he shouted, surprising even himself. "You deserve someone who's not a complete screw-up. Look at me, Sara. I've ruined everything."

Tears welled up in her eyes. "David, you're not a screw-up. You've made mistakes, but that doesn't mean you can't fix them. Let me help you."

He shook his head, feeling a lump in his throat. "No, Sara. I can't drag you down with me. I'm not good enough for you. I never was, and I can't be the reason you fall apart, too."

Sara stepped closer, her voice firm. "That's not your decision to make. I'm here because I care about you."

David's resolve wavered as he saw the pain in her eyes. He wanted to reach out, to pull her into his arms and tell her everything. But fear and self-loathing held him back.

"Just go, Sara. Please."

She stood there for a moment, tears streaming down her face, before turning and leaving the room. As the door clicked shut behind her, David felt an emptiness settle over him. He had pushed away the one person who truly cared, all because he couldn't see past his own failures.

Everything was too great for her to handle, so all she knew to do was pray. Pray in the name of Jesus, who was the greatest comforter. The greatest healer, the greatest redeemer, the Lord of lords and King of kings. It was only so much she could do, but He could do it all.

Epilogue

The school year had ended in a way no one could ever imagine. Four friends set out on their journey together, ready to take on what might, but what came were demons none had faced before—so they had no clue how to fight them.

Lewis, the humble gentleman, had been introduced to an ugliness that divided people. It could make you feel anxious, fearful, dehumanized, angry, and exhausted all at once. He grew up thinking life was one way, but he realized that the rules were different for him and not in his favor. This demon shows its face through stereotypes, microaggressions, and violence. A demon named Racism.

David, the local charmer, never had to worry about being alone because his charm and basketball skills always kept a crowd around. He didn't really know who he was without them. He allowed the demon to ride his back as he felt the weight of it and allowed it to psyche him out of something that could have been. A demon named Rejection.

Ashley, who was voted Best Smile and Life of the Party in high school, wasn't smiling anymore. What should have been a night of fun, a night to release stress, turned into an invisible wound that had scared her for life. But what took her joy wasn't just what happened that night but the demon that came with it. The one that whispered to her that she was unworthy and broken. A demon named Shame.

Sara, the faith-filled one who'd always known the love and support of her parents, was taunted by voices whispering, *"You'll always care more than they do,"* and *"If you love them enough, they'll stay."* She had overextended herself, confusing friendship and relationships with self-erasure. Those voices forced her to confront the difference between godly love and self-sacrifice without wisdom. Overcompensation and Abandonment were her demons.

It wasn't until she faced those demons that she realized her faith was being tested. It's one thing to know the Word of God, but another to live it. Sara experienced things she never imagined. She had plans for her future, and moving to Georgia wasn't one of them. Heartbreak wasn't in her plans, nor was losing her best friend.

Proverbs 16:9 reminds us that 'we can make our plans, but the Lord determines our steps' (New Living Translation). We can plan our lives out, but it's the Lord who has the final say. While college wasn't how any one of them planned it, it is the very thing that we call life. It molds us, then challenges us in the very thing we thought was true. It takes a ride, and we can either embrace it and make the best of it or ride it out frantically, yelling to get, but receive no reprieve.

Life, according to whom?

Stay tuned to see how their lives unfold.

Readers Reflection

While this story is fictional, the struggles within it mirror real battles faced in the spiritual realm. The challenges of pain, loss, anger, temptation, and confusion are not merely emotional—they are spiritual. Each moment of hurt or unforgiveness can become an open door for the enemy to gain access to the heart. Jesus reminds us in *Matthew 6:14–15* (*NLT*), "If you forgive those who sin against you, your heavenly Father will forgive you. But if you refuse to forgive others, your Father will not forgive your sins." Forgiveness is not easy, but it is essential. It begins with a decision, then unfolds through a process—one that may feel uncomfortable and exposing, but it leads to freedom and peace when surrendered to God.

Many of the struggles seen in this story—whether insecurity, self-doubt, hatred, addiction, confusion, or the longing to be loved—reflect how the enemy distorts pain to separate people from God's truth. Self-doubt whispers that you are unworthy; anger convinces you that revenge will heal; lust and addiction promise comfort but leave you empty. Yet none of these can fill the space that only God's love was meant to occupy. *John 8:32* (*NLT*) says, "And you will know the truth, and the truth will set you free." Freedom begins when the lies of the enemy are confronted with the truth of God's Word.

Faith is not proven in moments of comfort but in seasons of testing. Just as pruning refines a plant, trials refine the heart. The process of pruning can feel painful because it removes what is familiar—relationships, habits, or ways of thinking—but God allows pruning so that new fruit can grow. *James 1:2–4 (NLT)* reminds us, "When troubles of any kind come your way, consider it an opportunity for great joy. For you know that when your faith is tested, your endurance has a chance to grow."

Healing is also a journey. It often requires facing the very wounds we'd rather leave hidden. But when brought into the light of God's presence, those wounds can no longer control us. Forgiveness, surrender, and grace become tools of restoration. God does not waste pain—He transforms it. What once was shame can become testimony. What once felt like defeat can become deliverance. *Psalm 34:18 (NLT)* says, "The Lord is close to the brokenhearted; He rescues those whose spirits are crushed."

Even when life's broken pieces seem scattered, God still sees the whole picture. His love reaches into every corner of the soul, calling His children back to wholeness. The journey is rarely easy, but every step toward healing is a step closer to Him. Grace covers the process, and His strength meets us in the weakness we try so hard to hide.

Prayer:

Heavenly Father, thank You for seeing beyond my pain and for Your gift of healing. Help me forgive myself and those who have hurt me, and to release what no longer serves Your purpose. Help me to trust You with what I do not yet understand. Teach me to see myself and others through Your eyes of grace. Help me know that your love is unconditional and that you love me despite my flaws. Strengthen my faith through every trial, and let Your love be the light that leads me into being healed, whole, delivered, and free. In Jesus' name, Amen.